SCARLETT
doesn't live here
ANYMORE

LINDA RUTH BROOKS

When returning to your hometown isn't home anymore...

GUM TREE
press

A catalogue record for this
book is available from the
National Library of Australia

NATIONAL
LIBRARY OF AUSTRALIA

Cover, text design, typesetting & interior design by *Linda Ruth Brooks*
Photo artwork: *Linda Ruth Brooks*

ISBN: 978-1-7642121-7-5
978-0-9808161-3-6
Fiction/crime/Humour/Family

Scarlett doesn't live here anymore is a work of fiction. Any similarity
between the characters in this book and real people, living or dead, is
coincidental.

Author

Linda Brooks lives in Adelaide. She writes nonfiction, poetry, fiction and short stories. She has published and illustrated children's books. She has a BA Hons in Creative Writing from Southern Cross University. She gained a publisher for her childhood memoir *A Curious & Inelegant Childhood.* She has written a nonfiction book on living with Asperger's Syndrome *I'm not broken, I'm just different* and a children's book *Callan the Chameleon* with contributions from Professor Tony Attwood.

Published in anthologies: 'Coastlines' 5, 6, 7 & 8 by Southern Cross University; 'Wood, Bricks & Stone'; 'Grieve', 'Third Wednesday Poets' and 'Longing for Solitude'. Awards: Rebecca Coyle Scholarship for Hons; first prize for The Legacy University Level Creative Writing Award; first prize in the Gabe Reynaud Creative Writing Award and the Mater Misericordiae Grieve Writing Award.

A registered nurse and advocate for disability in a previous life, Linda has a rich background in listening to the stories of others, never shying away from the darker, gritty tales. And yet, humour is never far away. Linda enjoys hearing from her readers (even if they've found typos):

lindaruthbrooks@bigpond.com

Author titles

Nonfiction:
I'm not broken, I'm just different
(on Asperger's with Professor Tony Attwood)
A Curious and Inelegant Childhood

Adult fiction:
Behind Whispering Hands
The Unprize
A broken hallelujah
Scarlett doesn't live here anymore
The Lost Stories of Lucida Meredith Carter
Under the Bracken Fern

Children's books:
A Tabby Never Forgets
Callan the Chameleon (Asperger's Syndrome)
Dusty Bunny's Very Important Job
Izzy & Pudding the Cat
I want a monkey!
Madam Iris Bigglesworth
The Banyula Tales - 6 stories
Who Stole Christmas?

Publisher of the anthologies:
We are Australian
The Great Australian Shed
Waltzing Matilda

"I look back over my shoulder and feel the presence of an intense young girl and then a volatile and disturbed young woman, both with high dreams and restless, romantic aspirations.

"I long ago abandoned the notion of a life without storms, or a world without dry and killing seasons. Life is too complicated, too constantly changing, to be anything but what it is.

"Manic-depression distorts moods and thoughts, incites dreadful behaviors, destroys the basis of rational thought, and too often erodes the desire and will to live. It is an illness that is biological in its origins, yet one that feels psychological in the experience of it, an illness that is unique in conferring advantage and pleasure, yet one that brings in its wake almost unendurable suffering and, not infrequently, suicide.

"There will always be propelling, disturbing elements, and they will be there until, as Lowell put it, the watch is taken from the wrist."

Kay Redfield Jamison, *An Unquiet Mind: A Memoir of Moods and Madness*

Contents

In the silence

The mist furled like sleepy serpents in the moonlight; the only movement in the stillness. The highway wound through unyielding hills. The ocean was an echo away. A yearning sky hung bleakly, lending an air of foreboding. The roar of a Mac truck gouged open the silence.

In the passenger seat, Bren stared into the dense shroud of the night, blinking back the fatigue that threatened to engulf her. It was a rare pleasure to join John on his coastal run. They'd been on the road nine hours, and they were only half an hour from home. It was John's maiden voyage as owner and not merely driver. His own man at last. After fifteen years they had finally bought the huge transport that would be their freedom from debt, their release from the early struggles of their life together.

An ethereal figure appeared on the road. For a brief second Bren's eyes connected with those strange lost eyes. Or was it hours? Then, a sickening thud. The apparition was thrown like a rag doll. Or was it an animal, please

God, thought Bren, let it be an animal. She heard a primal scream.

Much later, she would realise the guttural sound that terrified her, had come from her own throat.

Bren saw John's hands clench the wheel as he applied all his force to the brakes. The truck slewed across the road. There was a screech of metal gashing open. A rocky outcrop of the road stopped the truck from tipping on its side. The real world faded, a nightmare world prevailed.

Like a giant slain dragon the truck rested at last, heaving and sighing. The headlights were twin streams of eerie light that parted the dense darkness, lighting the tangled bushland. The ghostly silver gums were silent sentinels, unwilling witness to this night's terror.

The tearing and shearing over, Bren grasped desperately for John, fighting the billow of his airbag, wrenching it aside with numb fingers. Her heart thumped frantically. Her eyes met his. They were alive. But what of the strange creature in the moonlight?

John's door was pinned against the hard rock face. Wordlessly they scrambled out the passenger door, unspeakable fear mirrored in their eyes. Every muscle taut, they ran back to the bundle of rags, shadowed in darkness. Was it human? Was it alive?

Bren's breathing was ragged and torn as her throat summoned a moan from shrinking lungs.

Oh God! Oh God! It was a woman, or a child. With

hair as black as silky midnight. One look was enough. Too late. Too late. Crouching over the lifeless body, Bren turned, desperately reaching for John, her arm slicing through the icy air. Forcing her rubbery legs, she pushed up from the asphalt. Low moaning came from behind a large rock at the side of the road. Bren found John curled up—heaving, retching. His huge hands helplessly grasping tufts of his hair.

Cradling his face she turned his head towards her. It was too dark to see him clearly in the shadow of the rock. Holding him against her, she soothed him, as a mother would a child.

The truck exploded in a hail of fire and light, illuminating his face. Raw terror fought for domination in her husband's eyes as he lost consciousness.

It's her

The morgue cloth draped the body, leaving only pale forearms in view and the soft curves of the left side of her face, just a glimpse.

'It's her. My wife. Scarlett.'

The midnight brilliance of Scarlett's hair fell in lush curves, spilling onto the trolley, and falling. Hair that was still so alive, radiant.

Stiff with grief, Brady bent low and buried his face in her hair, salty tears mingling with her sweet smell. Her hands, still elegant, wore the pallor of death. Lifting her left hand, Brady kissed every finger, stopping idly to worry at the blue paint stain on her thumbnail that only yesterday had annoyed Scarlett.

The attendant coughed.

Brady stared at the covers.

'Better not, sir,' she said.

He looked up at the woman, seeing angst and pity. He would know pity now. It would dog his heels and be reflected in every face he saw.

4

The woman was poised, hands folded neatly in front of her. With detachment, he noticed that she was perfectly made up, golden hair immaculately coiffed in a tight roll. Brady bit back a stab of anger. His wife was in death's cold hand, her beauty destroyed, and yet standing before him was female perfection.

Brady sensed his father's hand on his shoulder. He calmed. Everything he felt was irrational. Would the world he was forced to endure ever make sense again?

'Her arms, they're fine...' He broke the silence.

'...there's no damage there...'

'But...'

'She didn't try to protect herself. I'm sorry.'

'Why?'

'There's no way of knowing, sir.'

Brady swallowed. 'It was quick then.'

'Yes sir, instant.'

'She didn't...'

'No sir, she didn't suffer.'

'Her clothes?'

'She was only wearing a nightgown, sir.'

Brady looked up at her startled, numb. 'But...'

Her engagement and wedding ring sparkled, at odds with her lifeless form. Tentatively Brady removed them – her hand was cold. They came off easily; Scarlett had lost weight over the past months. Pausing, he looked at her right hand, posed gracefully on her chest. There was a large ruby ring on her finger. He had never seen it before. Scarlett had obviously been wearing it when she died. But before that?

Something in Brady shifted. Another emotion fought with cold dread. He would have known if Scarlett's parents had given her the ring. Who? When? Stepping back, he felt fury. She had been distant. Had someone else been allowed into her world? His mind reeled. Turning swiftly, he collided with his father, Jim.

Jim gripped Brady's arm. 'You should take it, the ring.'

'But, I don't want...'

'I know. Today you don't. But...'

'But when? Who...?'

'Don't assume. You don't know—anything.'

Jim tugged the ring from Scarlett's finger, placing it in Brady's hand. It was smaller than the others – a perfect fit, unlike the others. Whatever its origin, it was a recent acquisition. Gently he folded Brady's hand around the rings and led him away, outside to the unfettered air, away from the clinical smells of the morgue.

Brady stumbled against the rasp of the brick wall, disoriented. The rings fell from his hand. Jim picked them up and steadied his son with brown knotted hands.

'Oh God, Dad. Ebony. How do I tell a twelve year old girl that her mother isn't coming home? How do I explain what happened when none of this makes sense?' Brady moaned, leaning into the agony that washed over him, knees bent, hands gripping his thighs.

'Let her sleep. Sit awhile.' Jim steered Brady to a nearby bench.

'What the hell happened, Dad? Scarlett must have been awake. She doesn't sleepwalk.' His voice faded. 'She never has.'

Brady's phone beeped. With stiff fingers he accepted the call. 'Brady Harcourt speaking.'

Jim leaned forward, his body tense.

Brady spoke in monosyllables, yes, no. 'We're at the hospital. Yes, my father is with me. Jim Harcourt. We're near the...' He turned to Jim.

'In the garden behind the chapel,' said Jim.

Brady relayed the information. 'It's the police. They're coming here. I hope to God they can tell us something.'

The sky was turning from charcoal to milky grey, hinting at pre-dawn. A generator throbbed to life, lights from the hospital flickered. A siren howled in the distance.

Brady jumped to his feet at the first sounds of clipped footsteps. A blunt-faced heavy-set officer with intense eyes introduced himself to Brady, expressed his sympathy and nodded in brief acknowledgement of his father. 'Jim'.

He delivered a calm recitation of the facts, scant as they were. One of the attending paramedics had recognised Scarlett, otherwise they would have struggled with her identity. No personal belongings had been found near the scene of the accident. A further search would be carried out in the morning. She had been killed instantly, she'd wandered onto the road in the path of a truck.

'You're not a local?' he asked.

'Yes, no ... I mean Noarlunga's my hometown, but my wife and I live in Sydney. We're here for the summer. With our daughter, Ebony.'

'How old's your girl?'

'Twelve.'

'Sorry son, tough break for a young girl. Hard on you all. You staying with your father? I can reach you there?' He handed Brady a card.

'Yes.' Brady leaned forward, his voice hardened. 'The driver?'

'Treated for shock at the scene.' The officer's eyes were hooded. He took out a notepad, flipped it open, asked the address and wrote it down with quick lean strokes. 'I'll let you get home to the family, Brady. I'll be in touch.' He shook their hands. 'Jim, my best to Betty.'

Ebony and Betty were huddled together on the couch, their pale taut faces etched with fear.

'I couldn't find you, Dad. Or Mummy. Grandma Betty said something happened...' Ebony read grief in her father's eyes, whispered 'no', stood up in agony and ran to her father.

'Steve's coming over,' said Betty. 'I phoned him.'

Brady nodded.

'Good girl Bett.' Jim stood in the doorway. He'd be glad of his brother's support. Steve and Brady were more like brothers than uncle and nephew. Steve was sixteen years younger than Jim, an afterthought.

'It was such a windy night last night,' said Betty, clinging to the rituals of normal conversation as if it would gather the threads of the tragedy and help her comprehend it. 'Close the door, Jim. We'd better see to some food.'

'Right,' said Jim, leading the way to the kitchen and watching Brady lead Ebony to the sofa.

Steve slipped in the kitchen door, his sun-bleached hair a tousled halo. 'Jim, talk to me bro, what happened?'

The two men sat at the kitchen table as dawn teased the room with pink shadows. Their voices mingled with the burr of the kettle and the clink of mugs as Betty fussed, stopping every now and then to wipe her eyes with a handkerchief of Jim's that she retrieved from a pocket in her apron.

'Sorry,' said Betty as she clattered a cup into the sink.

Steve came to her side. Her hands were trembling. 'Your hands are red, Mum. Did you burn them?'

'Burn them?' Betty stared at her hands as if they were foreign. 'I don't know what to do,' she said, 'it's all wrong.'

'Bett, sit down pet.' Jim pulled out a chair. 'She's in shock.'

Steve frowned. 'Is she going to be alright?'

Jim silenced his brother with a quick shake of the head. 'Here Steve,' he said, handing his brother a damp tea-towel. 'Better wipe off your fluoro sunscreen. There'll be no surfing today.'

'Thanks bro.' He rubbed at his face. 'What was Scarlett doing out so late in her nightie?'

'Best not to ask,' said Betty, lost in the horizon beyond the kitchen window, where the May bush tapped restlessly on the glass pane. 'Best not. Too many hard questions.'

Steve raked Jim with anxious eyes.

'Don't mind Bett, Steve. She was like this after we left the farm. She'll come good.' Jim leaned back in the chair, sweat beads forming on his forehead. He was a short, hard muscled man with skin mottled by the sun. He paused. 'That is the question though isn't it...' his tone was flat, 'Hardly important now.'

Brady and Ebony entered the room, bound as one. Betty rose and gathered her granddaughter in her arms, her eyes steely with determination. She was needed.

Steve and Brady embraced silently.

Steve let his hand rest on Brady's shoulder. 'Phone calls, mate. We'll need to sort that.'

The next day Scarlett's red coat was found on the verge of the highway near the bushland. It lay in huddled perfection, as if it had been shrugged off, or fallen loosely. Its discovery provided a clue of sorts, but also muddied the waters. Scarlett must have been awake. She'd taken her best wool coat, but then discarded it. There was talk. It was a small town. Scarlett had been visiting galleries and attending art classes, the mania rising. She was painting prolifically at the studio of a young artist whose rising star drew many to his classes.

Ebony became Brady's pale shadow, refusing to leave his side, only eating or drinking when reminded, only dressing with her grandmother's help.

Scarlett's body was transferred to Sydney.

Brady organised for the return of their hire car, Steve insisted they fly to Sydney as a family, somehow managing to get five seats on the same flight.

Scarlett's parents, Tony and Elise Camberwell were stiff with grief. Their stoic formality wove them together, but built an impenetrable wall to the world. They were displaced, childless, lost. Tony wore desolation like an ill-fitting suit. He was crushed beyond caring.

Then the rituals of mortality: a rain-soaked funeral near her Camberwell ancestors, a cello soloist, a priest, murmured phrases, blood red roses. Faces drifted past, some remembered, some not. Hands clasped.

Brady was robotic, Ebony inconsolable.

The sun rose the next day, but its glory was wasted on Brady and Ebony.

Jim and Betty left, but Steve stayed for a fortnight,

sharing the dread of the phone calls, the questions and the grief. Then the balm of his presence was gone.

The numbness that had deadened the pain for Brady and Ebony deserted them like misty strands and a new form of grief shrouded them as they stumbled into a new version of their lives.

It was several weeks before the inquest was held. In this case it was a simple formality; no courtroom was convened. The findings were unremarkable, delivered first by phone and then a certificate was issued. "Accidental death occasioned by MVA (motor vehicle accident)". No fault was designated to the truck driver, John Burnside, who had been accompanied by his wife, Brenda.

Winter fell without the prelude of autumn. Summer lingered by the presence of storms and inner-city flooding. Brady haunted the guest bedroom, then chastened by his resistance to face life he vowed to sort the house, deal with the past.

Ebony saw his bumbling efforts to pack boxes of Scarlett's things. 'I can help Dad, let me.'

They walked into Scarlett's studio. There were canvases in various stages of completion. Her brushes and tools of the craft were scattered just as she'd left them. They clung together, overcome with emotion.

All their intentions of creating order were pushed

aside. This was Scarlett's sacred domain, a place that held more of her essence than any other corner of the house. Wordlessly they packed her art away before closing the door with a choking sob.

But memories clung deeper, surfacing in the night stretches, bringing Scarlett back. Brady had an ambiguous relationship with his dreams, having no choice whether contentment or chaos returned in the seasons of slumber. Would Scarlett arise in bleak despair or would she come with the joy of their early days? Would she bring those first tender kisses?

Hello

'When they said to be here at 9.00 am *sharp* for registration they could've told us we'd be lined up with a few thousand students. We could've come prepared with a few days' meals and deck chairs.' The girl's dark hair rippled as one slender foot tap-tapped the floor.

Her companion in the queue, a curvy redhead, didn't look up from her enrolment guide. 'They did warn us at orientation last night, Scarlett. You'd remember if you hadn't spent so much time flir...*chatting*.'

'I know they said we'd have a long day of it Carla, but you'd think they could organise enrolment for Fine Arts at a different time to the bloody boring finance prats.' The dark-haired girl folded her arms.

The queue noisily snaked across the auditorium, spasmodically spilling students at one of the dozen or so desks manned by staff that processed forms and answered questions, some with bright smiles, others with tired resignation. Behind the two girls, Brady flinched as the brunette's voice carried through the crowded auditorium.

14

He held his book higher in front of his face. He'd entertained a similar thought, but the grating rudeness of the girl in front of him banished any feeling of solidarity.

'Hey Scar,' called a deep male voice. 'Let us in with you.'

Brady looked up in disgust to see a smiling young man in a football pullover addressing the girl. He was accompanied by two scruffy friends carrying bulging canvas backpacks.

'Course Jase.' The girl waggled a finger in mock reproach. 'Did you sleep in, Lazy Bones?' She moved aside to allow them into the queue. Turning to Brady, she slowly pulled his book down and said silkily, 'You don't mind, do you?' A practised smile accompanied the words.

Brady glared. Of all the obnoxious tricks! The girl was a stunner. Her dark hair fell in a radiant sheet to her waist. That alone made her stand out. He knew her type—all looks and charm, used to getting everything she wanted. She waited for him to respond. A tense silence followed.

'Aw, come on mate,' said the short solid guy. 'You know how to be a gentleman to a lady, don't you?'

'Ah,' said Brady, turning to face the intruder square on. 'But you don't look like a lady, *Jase*. I have no intention of letting you and your mates jump the queue.'

Brady watched Jase clench his fists. Not for the first time, he was glad of his experience as an inner-city youth worker. The thick-muscled guy might have a physical advantage, but Brady was older and accustomed to dealing with thugs. This overconfident clown just out of school was no match for him. Brady stared him down. Jase allowed his friends to drag him away, giving a last backward juvenile sneer.

The girl's eyes widened. Dipping her head, she assessed Brady through thick lashes. 'I hate queues.'

'You don't say.' Brady's jaw clenched.

The loudspeaker system stuttered into life. 'Those students who *were organised* and attended yesterday's pre-enrolment session *and* completed their information packs then, may now proceed to the table at the far end of the hall.'

'That'd be right,' the brunette fretted, shrugging a negligent shoulder. 'Look, I'm sorry, I have the patience of a flea. Anyway, I'm Scarlett Camberwell, art student.' The ornate bracelet on her hand tinkled as she stretched out a silky hand.

Brady snapped his book shut, took her hand and gave it a firm shake. 'I'd love to stop and chat, Scarlett Camberwell, art student,' he said, 'but...'

'Oh. Right. You're one of the...'

'...organised ones who came yesterday? Yes, actually.' Brady slipped the book into his briefcase and turned to leave. He paused and looked back. 'How remiss of me, I do beg your pardon—the name's Pratt.'

The girl glowed.

Brady's eyes narrowed. He flashed a smile. 'But you can call me Boring.'

Lost without you

Tony and Elise Camberwell, Scarlett's parents, became pale visitors to Brady and Ebony, slipping into their lives with awkward movements. Tony was distant and restless, while Elise persevered with gaunt liveliness, attempting to create mundane conversations to cover the yawning chasm of family loss.

They dipped into Ebony and Brady's lives with the timidity of early morning swimmers finding their toes recoiling from water's wintry chill.

At first Ebony resisted their over-bright suggestions of outings and visits, then encouraged by her father she began to call in to see them after school.

Winter blended its dreary days with city smog, as Ebony's footsteps dragged on the pathway to the door. Her grandparents were both there, with eager faces and expectant voices. Sometimes she stayed for the evening meal, when at least the act of eating constructed part of the ritual of family. Inevitably family photos were brought out in a last grab to keep Scarlett alive in her daughter's mind. It was an understandable ritual, but still it cloyed, adding pressure to Ebony. It was a map of their own grieving, desperately shared. However, it couldn't be transplanted, or grafted.

Everything had changed.

Gone were the light days of popping in unannounced, finding Elise at work, Tony in his office and joining in whatever was happening. Ebony wondered about their lives. They no longer spoke of friends, work, parties or pleasure. Only of Scarlett. Ebony felt more of a ghost than her mother. The questions she longed to ask stayed buried. What had her mother been like? Before? Had she once been young and carefree? When had the darkness of bipolar begun? How? Her grandparents' reminiscences gave sanitised glimpses.

Tony and Elise shrank into the new construct of their lives. Ebony seemed distracted when she was with them. They saw her eyes graze the photographs and papers they offered as she stared at magpies dipping and swaying in the birdbath or was mesmerised by the swish of the cat's tail.

'Are we pushing her, do you think, Tony?' Elise was a tall woman with chiselled beauty that had sharpened into tired lines and shadows. She flipped open her cigarette case.

'You're not going to smoke in here are you Elise? I thought you'd given it up.' Tony flicked the newspaper upright with a crisp snap.

'Was Scarlett the only thing that held us together, Tony?' Elise crushed the cigarette into the ashtray, even though she hadn't lit it.

'Why all the questions, Elise? You never liked any of my questions. I was the worrier, the overprotective one. Why pull everything apart now?'

Elise crossed her legs and began to tap the air with her foot. Impotent anger flitted across her face. She picked up a magazine and flicked the pages noisily.

Tony sighed, dropped the paper and looked up. Their eyes met, then afraid of what they saw in each other, they glanced away. Tony slumped his head into the comfort of the lounge and closed his eyes.

The following morning Scarlett flew down the stairs, eyes bright. She sat opposite her father at the polished mahogany table that dominated the dining room.

'Hi Dad,' she said, pouring coffee into a mug.

'I hope you're going to have more than a cup of coffee, Scarlett.'

Scarlett grabbed a bagel and tossed it onto a plate. 'Mum wouldn't like you reading the paper at the table Dad.'

'She's at work. What she doesn't know, won't hurt her.' Tony Camberwell lowered his newspaper. 'Did you want to chat, sweetie?'

'I've met someone, Dad,' She hacked a thick slice of butter and grazed it across the roll.

Tony tapped the table with slender fingers. 'I thought something was afoot when you graced me with your presence for breakfast. I'm listening...'

'I've met a *man*.'

'A man?' Tony Camberwell's eyes narrowed.

Scarlett flushed under his gaze. 'Yes,' she said, steely challenge in her voice. 'A wonderful man. The man I'm going to marry.'

Tony Camberwell sighed heavily.

'Don't you believe me, Dad?'

'Oh yes, I believe you! The poor sod doesn't stand a chance against my beautiful, wilful enfant terrible. When did you meet Mr Wonderful?' Tony's appetite was diminishing.

Scarlett ignored the question, instead she embarked on a glowing, if somewhat sketchy description of Brady. 'He's so mature, Dad—he's in his last year at Uni. And he's been running a youth centre. He's a good man.' Scarlett hesitated, careful not to reveal that most of her knowledge of Brady had been gleaned through friends and websites. 'Anyway, he's the yin to my yang, whichever way that goes.' She waved a negligent arm. 'I can't imagine ever being down again, not like before. I mean, I was just a kid then, only fifteen. Yes, it was horrible, ghastly even, but you and Mum don't have to worry. Nothing like that's going to happen again. I'm fine, I'm an adult now.'

Tony Camberwell fought a spark of rising panic. They'd been through this before, their lives revolving around Scarlett's mercurial moods. His throat constricted at the memory of her first depressive episode. It had come after a period of euphoria.

'When will we meet him? I mean, your mother and I...'

'Soon,' Scarlett picked up her backpack.

'You're going? You haven't eaten.'

'Oh Dad! I don't have time.' Scarlett bent down and planted a generous kiss on her father's forehead, before running out the door.

Tony picked up his mobile and dialled his wife. 'Your daughter's in love, Elise,' he said.

'And you're concerned.'

'How can you tell?'

'Tony, we've been married a long time. You only refer to Scarlett as *my* daughter when you're worried or upset.'

'You know me too well. It's just happening too quickly, Elise. From what I can tell she's only had one conversation with this bloke and she's talking about love at first sight. She actually said, "I've met the man I'm going to marry".'

'She's a romantic. She's not the first person to say that, Tony.'

A tense knot formed in Tony's gut. 'But it's not rational, not really. And … well she was like this before. We know how that turned out.'

'You worry too much Tony. Scarlett has always been impulsive. At least she isn't depressed, that's a blessing.'

'But the higher she flies, the harder she falls.' Tony rubbed his temple.

'Nothing we can do darling. She has an artistic temperament, that's all.'

'I wish I had your sangfroid. I can't forget how she was before. Weeks in bed...I don't think I've ever been so afraid for anyone. I don't know why you're not concerned.'

'You worry enough for both of us, Tony.'

Stay

'I wish they'd stayed.' Betty massaged her back as she deftly flicked the rose heads she was pruning into a bucket beside her.

Jim rubbed the stubble on his chin. 'What do you mean Bett?'

'It was only supposed to be a year.'

Jim frowned. At times like this it was hard to keep track of where the conversation was headed. Even before Scarlett died she had been showing signs of stress. She'd had trouble sleeping and found it hard to concentrate. He found it best to wait, and let her go on.

Betty took her gardening glove off.

'Leave them on Bett, you know how your hands swell if you're scratched by the thorns.

'You're getting bossy in your old age, Jim. They make my hands hot.'

'Let's take a break, go inside and have a cup of tea.'

Betty wiped down a perfectly clean bench while Jim boiled the kettle.

'Earl Grey, Bett?'

'Yuk. I hate Earl Grey tea, Jim. You know that. It tastes like an old lady's purse. I'll have Irish breakfast, like always.' Betty kept up a rhythm with the cloth on the benchtop. 'Why did they have to fly Scarlett's body back? We have perfectly good cemeteries here.'

Jim took the cloth. 'You'll wear the bench out Bett. It was Scarlett's wish, Bett. They were only here on holiday.'

'I wish we'd never let Brady have that gap year. He was only supposed to be in Sydney for 12 months. Get some experience at that clinic place.'

'Youth centre.'

'Whatever. It was only supposed to be a year. Then it was Uni. Then he met that girl. And it was all over.'

'What do you mean all over?' Jim took the cleaning cloth from Betty's hands. 'Come on pet, your tea's ready.'

'Our chance to have our son near us again. Marrying her put an end to that. It was everything I was afraid of. We've only seen him a few times a year if we're lucky. And our granddaughter. She might look like her mother, but she's so much like Brady it isn't funny.' Betty began to sob.

Jim patted her hand. 'Come on Bett.'

'I hated getting on that plane. Taking them back to Sydney. So far from us again. I just wanted to scream. Stay with us.'

'I've missed them too.' Jim cleared his throat. 'It's not anyone's fault.'

'No, but it's so hard. And now it's even harder. To see our son torn apart by grief, and not to be there for him.'

'They have a life there. We'll just have to visit more often.'

Betty threw down the tea towel with a slap. 'We said that before, but the time was never right, or if it was we had to come when we were invited. Stay where we were told, leave when it was *convenient*.'

'Scarlett adored Brady, Bett. And she doted on Ebony. It wasn't easy for her either.' Jim pushed his chair back. It made a screech on the tiled floor. 'She was good to us too, Betty. Always kind.'

'You're pushing this devil's advocate thing a bit too far, Jim. You could try and understand. I told you we'd have a part time son. And that's what we got!'

'We can't change anything.'

'I don't have to like it.' Betty stood, dumped her untouched tea into the sink and went outside, letting the screen door slam behind her.

She lay on the grass and wept. 'I'm sorry Scarlett,' she whispered, 'but I loved him too.'

Jim and Betty had arrived a few days before the wedding.

After being shown their rooms, they sat in the formal lounge room, while the bridal preparations took on a life of their own. Scarlett was grace itself to the Harcourts— when she was around, which wasn't often. Betty watched

Brady. His questions were answered with lightning kisses. Scarlett all but vetoed his involvement in secret women's business.

'I thought that was just the dress,' he said, 'I *am* the groom.'

'You're studying for exams, darling...anyway, you should be pleased—all this is so boring for guys. And it's not a dress, it's a bridal gown,' said Scarlett, as she prepared for another shopping excursion with her mother, who gave every appearance of being as excited as the bride.

'Bye dears,' said Elise, linking her arm through her daughter's and throwing them a happy kiss. 'Do make yourself at home Betty, Jim.'

Scarlett wrapped herself around Brady and kissed him thoroughly. 'Don't wait up,' she giggled as she ran out the door to join her mother.

'So this is how the rich and famous live,' said Jim, earning a poke in the ribs from Betty.

'We're happy for you, Brady,' said Betty, kissing her son and looking him over with obvious pride.

'This thing a royal wedding?' asked Jim, when yet another huge delivery was made to the house.

'Jim, honestly,' said Betty.

'Well, a man doesn't want to look a dill at his own son's wedding. I just want to know if I should wear a tux and get you some new clobber.'

'Don't be silly, Jim. It won't be that formal,' said Betty, then seeing Brady's face flush added, 'Oh. Yes, dear. I think you may be right. Perhaps we will go shopping. I'd like to visit that Queen Victoria shopping place. Prudence Wainwright is always banging on about it.'

'Prudence Wainwright!' said Jim, 'we're not in her league either.'

'Who's Prudence Wainwright?' asked Brady.

'Earl Wainwright's wife, he's a solicitor. Gossipy old biddy, above the rest of us,' said Betty.

'She's been in a good paddock that one.' Jim blew out his cheeks and widened his eyes.

'Earl Wainwright. He used to come to the school and talk about being a council member. Sharp mind. Is he the one going for Mayor?'

'He would be, if he listened to Prudence, but frankly I don't think he cares one way or the other. He's a member of the local council. Real nice bloke actually, does a lot of good in the community,' Jim said.

Betty tapped Jim on the leg. 'Would Scarlett's mother like me to do anything, Brady?'

'Don't ask the boy that, Bett. Blind Freddy can see who's driving this wagon.'

'Well, I just thought I might be able to help with seating or something. You know, for the reception, they might want to know where to put our rellies. It's polite to offer, Jim.'

'The way Scarlett and her mother yak in the kitchen tells me they, er, have it all under control, Bett. So you and I might just as well relax.'

Brady shot his father a grateful look. After all, his mother hadn't heard the earlier conflict in the kitchen when Scarlett's mother had asked why Carla wasn't on the guest list.

Betty smiled. 'I relax shopping. We women are good like that.'

Jim moaned.

'I'll come with you,' said Brady, 'I'm obviously unnecessary too.'

Scarlett called out to Brady. He shrugged. 'Sorry Dad, I would've liked to keep you company while you waited for Mum. Here's a card for the men's outfitters where we guys are hiring our suits. They'll fix you up with something.'

'Thanks, son. It'll save me getting a second mortgage to buy a fancy-shmancy suit.'

Betty went to gather her coat and purse.

Jim turned to Brady. 'Hey son, what was the commotion about? Not that it's any of my business, but a bloke doesn't want to put a foot wrong if he can help it.'

'Not sure I want to know myself, Dad. Scarlett's fallen out with her friend Carla, the redhead I was telling you about.'

'I thought they were thick as thieves,' said Jim.

'So did I,' said Brady. 'They've been friends for years.'

'Women.'

Jim refused the offer to take Brady's car, declaring a lifelong love of train travel. He held Betty's hand as she dabbed at her eyes while the train rattled the few stations to the city. 'What's wrong, Bett,' he asked.

Betty sighed. 'It's just that I have the feeling that after the wedding we'll only have a part-time son.'

Scarlett was at her radiant best, floating down the aisle on her father's arm in a frothy gown that spoke of tradition. The service was formal and austere.

'They must have raided the Botanical Gardens,' muttered Jim, awed by the number of floral displays. He waited for a 'shush' from Betty, but she merely said, 'They probably own the Botanical Gardens, Jim.'

Where is home?

The dark sky opened and dropped another ocean of rain on the Sydney Harbour Bridge commuters. Falling in dense sheets, it obliterated the road. Brady clutched the steering wheel in frustration. The traffic was at a standstill, for what seemed like the hundredth time on this endless journey. He stared at the mobile phone, willing it to ring again. His stomach churned. The earlier phone call from the school was supposed to reassure him, but it had only produced more anxiety.

Ever since Scarlett died, Ebony had lost her vibrant glow, her spark. The cheerful banter that brightened his evenings after a long day at the office was a thing of the past. His daughter had been forced to grow up overnight. And now she had injured her ankle at school. How would she get on and off the train? The principal, Ms Prescott had tried to reassure him, but the mobile phone cut out right after the words, 'Don't worry, she's...' Why hadn't Ebony phoned him? Where was she? If today's traffic was like the last few days, it would take him two hours to make the journey home.

'I can't do this anymore.' The sound of his voice startled him. 'I can't.'

The outburst galvanised his thoughts. He'd been agonising over a solution for months and now he glimpsed one. He would sell their North Shore home and return to his hometown. God knows, he could do with the solace of family.

It would be a new home for him and Ebony, a new start. Away from the shadows of the past. He could renovate their beach house and put money aside. Scarlett's medical costs and hospitalisations had taken their savings. His income barely covered their lifestyle and Ebony's private schooling. Between work and commuting, he was hardly ever home. He missed family life. He'd never intended to join the rat race.

The ringing of his mobile interrupted his musings. It was Ebony. Quickly accepting the call, Brady was grateful the traffic was stationary.

'Dad, it's me.'

'Thank goodness, honey. Are you alright? Ms Prescott said...'

'Oh, Dad, I'm fine, Prescott always overreacts. I'm home. It's just a sprain. Leisa and Ben helped me on and off the train...'

'But how did you get home from the train station?'

'Dad, you worry too much. Old Mrs Petrie from next

door had been shopping, she's always on the same train as me, you know that. She insisted on getting a taxi for us. Honestly, I'm not a baby. I can look after myself, you know. I've been doing this for years.'

'But you're injured. Why didn't you call me? I would have come for you.'

'Sure! And how long would it take you to get here? Look, I'm okay. The school nurse said I only need to stay off it for a week. Lucky exams are over.'

'We need to talk when I get home, but I'm in the car now...'

'You'd better get off the mobile then, Dad.'

'See you la...'

Ebony had signed off.

Brady fussed over Ebony's in-flight luggage at gate 51.

'Dad, leave that alone. You're embarrassing me!' Ebony flushed red. 'You've checked it like a hundred times.'

'Sorry, Bub.'

'And don't call me that!'

'I wish you would wait for me. I'll be finishing work in two weeks.'

'We've been through all this, Dad. Grandie will meet me. I've flown on my own to Adelaide before, it's not even two hours in the air. I'm not going to Alaska.' She flicked the ticket into her purse. 'Unfortunately.'

'Unfortunately? What does that mean?'

'Did it ever occur to you that I might be less than thrilled with this seachange of yours?'

'What do you mean—my seachange?'

You can't be serious! *We* haven't talked about this. When did you decide? Did you just wake up one morning and think "Hey, let's move to my hometown?" What's wrong with you? It's not like you to have half-baked ideas. How do my feelings figure in this?'

'I thought you'd be happy. Every New Year's holiday with Nan and Grandie you've said you wished we lived there. You're always complaining about trains and school.'

'That's not the point!'

'Well, pardon me if I'm confused.'

'Jeez, Dad. You are such a...a bloke.'

The steward announced that the plane was boarding.

'Goodbye, Dad!' Brushing his cheek briefly with her lips, Ebony snatched her backpack and joined the queue.

On the plane she slumped into the seat, grateful she had a window seat. She had the row to herself, so she put her backpack on the middle seat.

As soon as the plane landed, she bounded from the seat, flung on her backpack and stood stiffly in the narrow corridor waiting for the queue of passengers to move.

She arrived breathlessly at the luggage carousel and tripped over her backpack. 'Oh, crap!' she muttered.

'Is that any way to greet your dear old grandfather?' said Jim, hugging her. 'Welcome home, Ebony.'

'Hi Grandie. I'll have to get used to calling this place home, I guess.' Ebony stepped towards her suitcase, but her grandfather lifted it off the carousel with ease. 'Where's Gran?'

'She's a bit tired, pet. She doesn't get out as much as she used to, but she'll be thrilled to see you.' Jim wrapped his free arm around his granddaughter. 'You can't believe how happy I am to have you. Is this all your stuff?'

Ebony rolled her eyes. 'Of course not Grandie. The rest of the stuff is arriving with the removal guys tomorrow.'

'Don't tell me your dad's leaving the unpacking up to you?'

'No such luck, Grandie. I'm not allowed to touch anything until Dad comes in two weeks. Apparently, I'm still a child.'

Changed

Brady threw his backpack casually over one shoulder and alighted from the plane with loose limbed ease. He scanned the airport lounge for Steve and jumped when a thump on his back alerted him to Steve's presence.

'Shit, Steve! Where'd you come from?'

'Be thankful I came at all, nephew. What possessed you to arrive at 1 am?'

'Loose ends at work. Don't ask.' Brady looked around. 'Ebony not here?'

Steve narrowed his eyes. 'No, she said it was past her bedtime.'

'So, is she going to be at the cottage?'

'Don't you talk to your daughter, Brady? What are you asking me for?' Steve led the way to the baggage claim area. 'Is everything okay with you two?'

Brady shrugged. 'I dunno. Teenagers.'

Steve raised an eyebrow. 'Go on. You two get on like a house on fire. Just us against the world and all that.'

'Not so much lately. I don't know if she's ever going to

forgive me for moving back to Noarlunga.'

'Ah, right. Gotcha. Fifteen-year-olds are hard to transplant I hear.'

Brady grunted and lunged for a suitcase. 'That one too, Steve. Yeah, that's it. Thanks, mate.'

Steve slipped the gym bag Brady had indicated from the carousel. 'I'll tell you one thing for free, Brady. Jim and Betty are absolutely thrilled.' He led the way out the glass doors. 'But they might not show it. They're afraid you might change your mind and go back.'

'Well, that's not going to happen. Why would they...'

'You've been gone a long time, mate.'

'But surely...'

'You were only going to Sydney for a year in the first place, remember?' Steve flipped open the boot of his 4WD and threw the cases in.

'What are you trying to say, Steve?'

'Things change, Brady. People, places.'

"Course. I know that.'

They spent the short journey in silence.

'You awake, mate? I've set up a bed for you. Even chucked some sheets on it.' Steve grinned. 'And I've plugged in the fridge so we can have a cold beer while you wind down from the rat race.'

'Thanks. Is that all that's in the place. Beer?'

'Pretty much. Although there might be some stale pizza.'

'Oh great. I thought Ebony…'

Steve shot Brady a sideways glance. 'She said you vetoed her from unpacking. Besides there's a mountain of boxes. Anyone would think you'd brought all of Scarlett's stuff as well.'

Brady was silent.

'Oh crap. Don't tell me you did!'

'I never got 'round to sorting it.'

'You're kidding me. You're a lost cause, sunshine.'

'I'll get around to it. It's not a big deal.'

'If you say so, but it looks like your baggage isn't just stuff in boxes. You'll have to face it sometime. Unless you intend setting up a museum.'

'That's a bit harsh. There's a lot of memories in those boxes.'

Steve took a torch from the glovebox and handed Brady a key. 'Okay, mate. Let's christen this new home of yours. Don't trip over the…'

Brady stumbled. 'Ouch, what the hell?'

'It's a duck. Apparently Ebony made it in pottery at school and gave it to Betty. She's had it in the shed and thought it would be good to welcome you.'

'Crikey, that doesn't sound like Mum.'

'Things change, Brady.' Steve shone the torchlight on the path.

'If you say that again I'm going to clock you.' Brady limped to the door. 'That bloody duck is the size of an emu.'

'It's good luck. Feng Shui or something.'

'Yeah, I see how that works! Probably broke my foot.'

'You'd better have two beers, you miserable git.' Steve laughed and followed Brady into the cottage.

Brady flicked the light switch and glanced around. 'Oh fair go, Steve. I thought you said you'd made a bed up for me!'

'I did.'

'It's a bloody canvas camp cot!' Brady dropped his back pack.

'Welcome home, sunshine.'

'It's going to be a long night,' said Brady, hoping dreams of Scarlett didn't intrude. He was tired of being thrust into the past while he slept.

But his hopes were dashed.

As he tossed on the small camp cot, misty dreams of Scarlett invaded his sleep as soon as he drifted off. Scarlett laughing in the surf, dancing in the rain with Ebony, crying over a pet mouse, shrouded in the morgue. She wandered the rooms of his mind at will. She became ephemeral as the dreams collided, and Scarlett moved faster, her feet off the ground, floating, surreal as dawn approached.

Brady broke into a sweat as he struggled to find Scarlett and bring her down to earth. She laughed and rose higher. His heart thundered. Scarlett flung clothes as she flitted through echoing rooms. Brady strained for her, calling her name.

The first whispers of spring promised a warm summer. Brady and Scarlett were the last of the group left at their favourite restaurant, and the last patrons in the outdoor gazebo. The group had left noisily for a local bar, a situation that had taken some planning on Scarlett's part. Carla had been in on the ruse and left in a flash of jade taffeta, giving Scarlett a quick wink before ushering the others away.

With Brady steadily holding her gaze, Scarlett sensed a new awareness in him as he reached out to curl a tendril of her hair around his finger. 'You add light and shade to my world,' he said.

Scarlett held her breath. She had never felt so close to anyone, to anything—so close to something real. It had taken her months to become a part of Brady's world. Brady reached out with deliberate hands and cupped her face, drawing her closer. Claiming her mouth with his, he began a slow lingering kiss.

Scarlett trembled, then, sliding her hand under Brady's shirt, she was rewarded with a sharp intake of breath. She sensed his surrender. He drew her closer still, his hands roaming the silky skin of her neck.

They made love that night, tumbling around her room amid clothes, paints and textbooks. Scarlett felt like a goddess who had pulled the stars closer to earth, one who'd brought Brady not only to her, but to himself. They talked all night as their need for each other became love, passionate, sweet; excluding the world. They were two. They were one.

Chasm

'You don't like them do you?' Ebony crossed her arms as she regarded her father through piercing eyes. It was an accusation. She hated the words, but she was confused.

In the doorway to her room Brady dragged weary fingers through his dark unruly hair.

Ebony experienced a flicker of guilt as pain washed over his face. They had been unpacking all day and they were both wrung out, but she stood her ground. He'd brought them here. She was fifteen, not five. Even the pretence of a choice would have been better than this, this overnight upheaval. She saw her father's eyes slide away from the row of images. It was the last straw that he couldn't even bear to look at photographs of her mother.

'No, I don't,' Brady agreed at last.

Ebony shrugged. 'I don't get it. They're beautiful—*she's* beautiful. Is it because another man took them? Is that it?' She was pushing him, but she couldn't stop.

'It's not that,' answered Brady, 'that just isn't the woman I remember.'

'Well, it is her. You just don't want to remember. She wasn't just yours, Dad. She was mine too—my mother. You can choose what you want to remember, but you can't tell me what memories to keep, or what pictures to have.'

Brady turned wordlessly and walked away.

Ebony closed the door, wishing she had the guts to slam it. Her father didn't understand. Why would he, he'd never known the charade she had carried out, trying to get her mother dressed and sitting up to an evening meal, telling her to smile and be happy, begging her to stop crying. Never having friends over because it was too hard to explain why her mother was still in bed in the afternoon, or that she was painting and couldn't be disturbed.

She was angry with her father for not knowing, even though she'd hidden so much from him too. Pretending her mother had made the meal and she, a young girl, had merely helped. Nobody knew. There was no way they could know. It was just the way things were. It was all Ebony had ever known. She'd tried to understand her mother's emotional landscape. She'd acted as if everything was okay, hoping that somehow pretence would become reality, but it hadn't, and she no longer knew who she'd been protecting. Maybe herself, at last.

The row of photos lined the wall of her room that faced the window. The evening shafts of light were gently filtered through yellowed gauze curtains, illuminating the black and white studies of her mother. They displayed her many moods. Ebony had been delighted when she found them in the tea chest when they were unpacking. Her father's reaction was instant, and surprising. He had been returning them to the depths of the tea chest when Ebony snatched them from him.

Reverently she traced a slim finger over each picture. There was one of her mother pirouetting in the froth at the edge of the surf, holding her flowing skirt out of the water's reach. Scarlett's hair was flying through the air, her face alight with laughter.

There was another where she was shielding her face with a partially finished painting, her body languid and graceful, as she leant on the door jamb to the art room at Uni. In another, she was solemn and intense as she bent over a desk, her hair tied high with a purple bandana.

The last picture was of Scarlett with her head resting on her hand, her reflection also captured in a rain spattered window with the backdrop of the dark night sky outside. Candlelight glowed in the room, softening the image in the windowpane. Two images in one photograph, one stark and sad, one blurred.

Kissing the sad face, Ebony grabbed her shawl. Heading into the fading light through the back door of the cottage that was now home, she nimbly ran down the steep incline and onto the beach. With one quick backward glance, she saw her father bent over the kitchen table. Folding the shawl around her, she ran along the beach, laughing into the wind. Let him unpack the bloody kitchen. Too long it had been her domain.

He wanted a sea change; he would get one.

There was a shadowy figure ahead. Ebony slowed to a walk, unaccountably annoyed with the intrusion to her solitude. The intruder was beach fishing, a tall slender silhouette, faintly illuminated by the last of the sun's rays as they disappeared behind the crowded cottages on the hill. Ebony looked back to their cottage and considered going back, but she didn't want to face her father yet.

She continued towards the stranger. It was her beach too. Like it or not, it was her sea change, courtesy of her father. A father who was showing all the classic signs of having a mid-life crisis.

The false courage generated from her rebellious outburst with her father dissipated as she approached the lone figure. The stranger was wearing an oversized checked flannelette shirt and a baseball cap worn backwards.

'Hi,' she said, wondering at her bravado. She'd never initiated a conversation with a stranger in the city as long as she could remember.

'Hey yourself,' said a lilting voice. The stranger met Ebony's eyes with a confident gaze. The stranger was a girl about her own age. 'I've been coming to this beach, like forever, and still can't manage to get the hang of this beach-fishing thing. You new here? You're not a local. I'd know if you were. I'm a sticky beak. Well, that's what Dad says. But really, that's rich coming from him—he's a PI, you know, Private Investigator. Used to be a cop. He asks questions for a living. What is it with fathers?'

Ebony's mind was spinning. Which question was she supposed to answer? She surprised herself by saying, 'Don't talk to me about fathers!' She had intended to start a polite conversation; how had she veered straight into this? Perhaps it was the complete naturalness of the girl in front of her.

'Huh. Yours too?'

'He's lost the plot,' volunteered Ebony. She might as well go with the flow. It was strangely freeing. 'He's walked out on a well-paid job, left a mansion on the North Shore and decided on a sea change.'

'So you didn't want to move?' asked the girl.

The girl's short blonde hair was spiking out at all angles from the cap. Ebony was mesmerised as the girl deftly threaded a prawn onto the hook and threw the line into the ocean with an elegant swing. She had the movements of a dancer.

'Huh?' said Ebony, hating that she'd lost the thread of the conversation.

'Did you like city life? I hated it, that's why I came to live with my dad. Mum's an actor.' The girl rolled her eyes theatrically as if no further explanation was needed.

'Well...I don't really like the city. Spent half my life on crowded trains, and pretty much hated my school. It was having Dad assume he knew best for us both. The first I knew of *our* seachange was a removal guy arriving to give a quote.'

'Ah, I get it. Treated you like a kid. Parents do that if you let them.'

Ebony's brow crinkled in confusion. 'If you *let them...?*'

'Well of course! God, you don't think they actually wake up one morning and start treating you like a responsible adult, do you? You have to make them listen. Me, I usually tell them stuff after I've done it. Like, for instance, I only told my dad I was leaving Mum's and coming to live with him when I was already on the plane.'

'Wow. What did your mum say?'

'Short version—good-bye, long version, you don't want to know. Like I said, she's an actor.'

'Oh,' said Ebony, struggling with the girl's attitude, but in awe at the same time. 'So you're over 18.'

'Oh cripes no! I'm 15.' The girl smiled. 'Anyway, I'm Jenna.'

'I'm Ebony.'

'Cool name, very arty. Your parents creative types too?'

'Well, Dad's an accountant. Mum was an artist, but she

died three years ago.'

'Oh right, the old opposites attract thing. Same for my parents. Oil and water. Sorry about your Mum, must be dreadful.'

'Yeah,' said Ebony. She warmed to the confident straight-talking girl. It was the first time in a long while someone hadn't been uncomfortable and apologised awkwardly for her loss. It was refreshing.

'Hey,' said Jenna, 'we might be in school together. How old are you? Are you going to Noarlunga High?'

'Yes, not that there's much choice,' said Ebony, smiling.

At her last school she never felt she fitted any group. Of course it didn't help that she'd given up inviting friends home, because she never knew how she would find her mother. Nervous and jittery, depressed and unkempt, or over-the-top manic, trying to be the coolest mother ever. Ebony didn't know which was worst. Or best.

'So, you went to a private school too. Every rule has a subset of rules. And every subset has amendments and subsections.'

'Pretty much,' responded Ebony, thinking this was a fair description of Grantham Hill Grammar. 'So why'd you decide to live with your dad? Wasn't it really cool having an actor for a mother?'

'*Oh pleeease!* It would be okay if she left the drama

queen act on the set. I don't know about your mother, but mine lives her craft. Everything takes second place to her being in the zone. Bloody annoying at the best of times. But then she was insulted at having to become a grandmother on the show, so she told them to take her out of the story line for a while. It's just a ploy. She's done it before. She won't leave; she's just trying to get leverage with the producers. It didn't work because they called her bluff and didn't renew her contract, so she decided to go to London and do the pantomime season. They love Aussie actors over there.'

'Oh, so that's why you came to live with your dad?'

'No. She won't be over there long. I'm here to stay. Of course, Dad doesn't know that yet. Better to ask forgiveness than permission, I reckon. He won't send me back. He's as big as a grizzly bear, but he's a softie. And he's so easy to be around. No drama, you know. His wife Helena is a sweetheart, which is more than I can say for Mum's latest paramour. Don't get me wrong, I love Mum, but a little goes a long way, y'know? My older sister Jaz takes after her.'

Ebony giggled. Jenna's home life sounded like a circus.

Wistfully, her eyes followed the fishing line out to the sea. Jenna's family seemed to scorn the pretence of a normal life.

Unlike her own, which rested on secrets and cover-ups to protect her mother's often fragile mental state. Well, that hadn't even worked. Her mother was gone.

'Jeez, you were miles away,' said Jenna.

'My mother was bipolar,' said Ebony, shocked by her uncharacteristic candour. In all the times she'd imagined sharing this news with any of her school friends, she'd rehearsed building up to the truth slowly. Perhaps that's why it had never happened.

'Yeah, I've heard of that. One of Mum's friends has it. Brilliant actor.'

Ebony smiled a rueful smile that was lost in the twilight. She'd shared a secret and it felt good.

It was late when Ebony returned.

Ebony crept silently into the dark cottage. Her attitude softened towards her father when she saw the photograph on the corner unit in the lounge. It was one of her favourites, the three of them at the beach, pink-cheeked and flushed with happiness. She touched it reverently, then crept into her room and fell asleep instantly.

You were

Brady flinched at the slamming of the door. He abandoned the thought of following Ebony and instead went to her room and sat awkwardly on her bed. The dying twilight strobed the room with shifting fingers of light and shadow. He stared at the images of Scarlett.

'I'm sorry, Scarlett,' he said. 'I'm sorry.'

He felt the bulk of paper in his pocket, the letter he had grabbed and hidden from Ebony. It was better that she thought he'd been trying to hide the photos, rather than have her see the letter Scarlett had written. The letter he found the morning after their wedding. He had merely skimmed it back then, kissed her forehead and thanked her. Their love was too large, too heady in those early days for him to measure and savour the words. Forever had been in their hands, the future was theirs, a gift without question.

Reaching into his pocket with a taut breath, he retrieved the letter and held it with both hands.

'I'm sorry I've forgotten those early days Scarlett, sorry

I've hidden from the beauty of you. I let anger and pride get in the way.'

Brady sighed and looked out at the descending fog that whirled like an intangible vapour. 'Do you see the mist, Scarlett? Just outside this window. They are all the tears I've cried, the wisps of memories. I can't touch them. If I go out to find them, they'll be gone. I will be a blind man wandering within a ghost. I'm not angry anymore. I want you to know that. But you're still a mystery I can't solve, a fog I can't escape. Funny. You always said you'd haunt me. Is that what this is? This heavy coat of grief I wear. Don't laugh ...I saw a therapist. Yes, me, the one who took you to your appointments. I was the one who wasn't broken or confused, the passenger in your life. But, you see Scarlett, now I'm the broken one. You want to know what the therapist said? "Don't hide from the past Brady." Yes, I thought you'd see the irony. "Go back and read Scarlett's love letters," he said, "read them aloud," he said. "There's only one," I told him. Stupid thing to say. Can you imagine that? I guess you understand better than I.'

Brady unfolded the letter and smoothed it on his knees. 'So here goes, Scarlett.'

My husband, Brady,

I like that—'husband'. I think it will be my favourite new word!

How I wish I'd had the courage to say our vows, or read

them to you. I thought I could, I really did. I polished and rehearsed the words. But then, on the day, it was all I could do to place my hands in yours and stop them from trembling. Then I messed it up when I looked in your eyes and said 'I love you forever' instead of 'I do.' Everyone laughed and I blushed and said 'I really do'.

You mean too much to me you see. I know that. You are my everything. People shrink from that extravagance, the hyperbole of the words. But you are. Everything. It's unrealistic, it's crazy, I know.

I heard what people said 'Oh, Scarlett is so dramatic, so over the top, so intense.' You never said that. You were the first one to ever treat me as if I wasn't tainted, defective. You never treated me as if I had a disease strapped on my back. A thing I could shrug off at will. You got on the Scarlett roller-coaster. You chose me. Or perhaps I chose you and you chose me back. Thank you for choosing me back.

I'm not that great with words, perhaps one day I will paint our love. Then you'll know.

Before you, love songs were jokes life played, mocking lyrics of joy I would never know, cruel anthems of steps I thought I would never dance. Before you, I walked in dark alleys where the sun refused to shine. I was going to tell you all about that, that's what this letter was going to be about. I was going to gently lead you through the shadows of my past. Open Pandora's box, share all the secrets of my soul. Hold nothing back.

But I looked into your eyes last night and realised I didn't need to go back. You love me, and know I love you. That my love is perfected by my imperfections. And if you ever come across my stumbling footsteps of the past I will trust you. Trust you to understand, to forgive. I trust you to know that you have the best of me, and always will.

With love, Scarlett, your wife (my other new favourite word!!).

Brady left his vigil at his bedroom window when the rustlings in his daughter's room ceased. She didn't hear his gentle tap on her door, nor did she see his soft gaze on her as he watched her sleep.

Silently closing her door, Brady returned to his bed where he lay awake 'til dawn.

Scarlett was a child-bride of conflicting excesses.

Fifteen months after they were married, she gave birth to Ebony. While pregnant, she was the picture of maternal contentment, but the onset of postnatal depression was swift and brutal after the birth. While spending eight weeks in a Karitane Mothercare facility she was diagnosed with bipolar. And, as Scarlett struggled with the condition, Brady realised he had to come to terms with a new version of their life together. A tight knot of worry shadowed his steps.

When the darkness of depression clung and shrouded

Scarlett, showing no sign of abating, Brady resigned from the youth centre, finding a job in the city closer to their home. Life became a sliding scale of negotiated compromise.

Scarlett dropped out of Uni soon after the wedding. 'Why should I study when I have you? Anyway, I can still study art privately and paint. I'd never give that up.'

She spoke casually, as if she was discussing a grocery list. She embraced art as a saviour. When mania lifted her above the mortal world she was prolific, creating rich vibrant canvasses, working all through the night. At the zenith—that brief plateau of mania where stillness momentarily preceded the next downward spiral, she embraced life with euphoric awe. Everything consumed her then, as she cleaned for days on end, then cooked— often filling the freezer; before digging up large areas of the garden.

The descent came with no warning, no gathering of storm clouds, no foresight. Scarlett clung to her brushes, cocooned in the studio, pushing for inspiration with the desperation of a mountain goat struggling for purchase on rocky ground, but still she spiralled, flailing, reaching; like a sky diver falling, grasping every tree branch on its way back to earth. When the darkness descended, she retreated to the womb of depression, spurning the easel, the brushes and the studio. They had betrayed her.

Brady often wondered if she was trying to balance out

the dead days by scrambling intently for the sunshine when she could. Did the highs cause the lows? (If only she could moderate them). He went to her specialist and learned her brain landscape was unique. His lovely, generous wife was clinging to normalcy, engaged in a war he could not join or comprehend—a war where she was courageous, a warrior. Sometimes he thought she loved the disease that both ravaged and enlivened her. At other times, she seemed to despise it and herself as both extremes struggled for dominance.

And yet, there were many seasons when Scarlett transcended the dark shadows.

From an early age Ebony had known at some level that her mother was different, but their life was the only reality she knew. She accepted her father's explanation that her mother didn't choose to be this way, she was merely a passenger. While neither of them could enter Scarlett's world at the peaks or the deepest valleys, they learned to wrap themselves around each other, and her, like a team of dancers, anticipating, responding.

Whether in the highs, the lows or the plateaux, she had been the centre of Brady and Ebony's world. After she died neither of them knew how to choreograph a new dance. Their best efforts to cling together fell short. Grief proved a stronger master. And the dull days of slow renewal found them estranged in odd little ways; awkward misunderstandings, lingering silences.

And then she was gone.

If Scarlett's life had been complex, her passing was even more so.

Life for Brady and Ebony had paused. They were like actors who had only been given the script for Act I and were expected to go on with Act II.

Who

'Quite a five o'clock shadow you have there, Brady.' Jim Harcourt raised a hand to block out the sun, as he assessed his son. 'I nearly mistook you for a removalist. You could've come and got me to help. I'm only next door.'

'The removalists came a few days ago.' Brady tugged at his beard self-consciously. 'It's not staying.'

'Who's not staying?' Betty tugged on Jim's arm.

'I must have been out when they came. You right Bett?'

'Did you check the mail, Jim?' Betty looked up to her husband.

'It's Sunday Bett.' Jim frowned as Betty bent down and tugged at weeds beside the path. 'How's the unpacking going son?'

'Well on the way, Dad.'

'Your lights were on till all hours. You could've asked for help. A man likes to feel useful, son. Especially to his own.'

Brady shrugged. 'Nice to see you too, Dad.'

'Hello, Grandie. Hi Gran.' Ebony giggled, hugging her

grandfather warmly while Betty smiled absently. 'How do you like Dad's beard? He's aiming for Soho Hippy.'

'Well he missed. He'd frighten the dead,' said Jim whisking Ebony into his arms. 'How are you settling in poppet?'

Brady sighed. 'We were just leaving for a walk on the beach. Then have lunch at the kiosk.'

'Oh, how lovely. A walk along the beach. What a wonderful idea,' said Betty. 'Did you bring my hat, Jim?'

Brady swallowed his frustration. Plans for time with his daughter were being derailed. He threw his father a beseeching look, but Jim was watching Betty like a hawk. 'Sure, we could all go.'

'Yes, Betty. Your hat is in the car with the golf bag.'

'Oh Jim, you know I hate golf,' Betty pouted, crossing her arms in childlike defiance.

'I wasn't going to play golf, Bett,' said Jim.

'Why can't you play golf Grandie? I'll come with you,' said Ebony. 'Dad can take Gran to the beach.'

She ran inside and came back with her iPod. Linking her arm through her grandfather's, she smiled at her father. 'You don't mind, do you, Dad.'

'He'd love it,' said Jim. 'I'll fetch your mother's hat and bag.'

Brady frowned. How was it that his father was in charge of his mother's purse and hat?

As Brady walked with his mother along the track

leading to the beach he could have sworn he heard Ebony say, 'Thanks Grandie, I needed rescuing from Dadzilla today.'

At the beach the only sounds that intruded were the rhythmic flapping of the umbrellas over the outdoor dining area, the distant caw caw of the seagulls with the soft slapping of the ocean on the shore in the background.

Brady and his mother sat on the whitewashed benches that faced the ocean. The sea carelessly lapped the bleached sand. The scene before them was idyllic, but it failed to bring the calm Brady desperately needed.

Moving into the cottage that overlooked the craggy cliffs had kept father and daughter busy. Unpacking and sorting provided Brady with a sense of control. Unfortunately, it proved to be short-lived. He'd been unprepared for Ebony's outburst over the photos. How could he explain that the woman in the photos was a reminder of the young woman who disappeared into another world? The unpredictable world of her mental illness. It wasn't even grief that made the photos unbearable, it was the sense he should have been able to do something. Make her keep taking her medication; something, anything.

Betty was the picture of contentment as she licked her ice cream. Try as he might, Brady couldn't remember his mother ever having an ice cream. She was in her own world, she'd hardly said a word to him on the walk there. The quiet was shattered by the laughing voices of a woman and child. They were rollerblading, hands entwined. The boy, who was about seven or eight, was concentrating so hard he gnawed his bottom lip. Wearing enough protective gear to start their own shop, they were different, but strangely in sync. The woman's movements were effortless, but she took great care to pace herself to the boy who was clearly struggling. She wore purple leggings and a bright multi-coloured mini skirt that swayed rhythmically as she moved, the colours of a gypsy, colours Scarlett would have worn. Brady's jaw clenched.

'I think that's enough for now Dylan,' said the woman gently, her voice a combination of richness and warmth. Taking off their helmets they sat at a nearby table.

'Will I ever be as good as you, Emma?' asked the boy, gazing up at the woman with innocent adoration.

'Of course you will,' she said, reaching down and massaging the boy's calf muscles. 'When your leg heals I won't be able to keep up with you.'

Looking away, Brady stared at the horizon, pushing back the image of the newcomer. Her tenderness to the boy had stirred a distant memory. Of a time when Scarlett was young and carefree, a time when he was the centre of her world, and the light of his daughter's days. He remembered how Ebony smothered him with kisses and begged for horsey rides on his back as soon as he walked through the door. How he longed to recapture those moments. He might have lost Scarlett, but he'd be damned if he was going to lose Ebony.

Brady dragged his attention back to the last of his ice-cream. He'd forgotten about it and sticky liquid was dribbling down his hand. His mother handed him a lace handkerchief. Really! She'd be wiping his face next.

The morning crowd was growing. A mother with a baby in a pram and a toddler had arrived noisily. The toddler began to chase the seagulls, shrieking with delight as they took to the air.

'There goes the neighbourhood,' muttered Brady. His mother stared at him and moved her chair away from him.

The woman looked up. She took off her sunglass and waved to Betty. 'Hello Betty, how are you? I hope you're not going surfing. You'll get your dressing wet. We have to look after that ulcer if it's going to heal properly.'

'Oh Emma, you're such a trick. As if I could ever surf! Couldn't do much more than dogpaddle, dear.' Betty rose and walked towards the two. 'May I sit here?'

'Of course, Betty. You're welcome,' said Emma. 'That's quite an ice-cream you have there.'

'That young man bought it for me.' She waved a nonchalant hand in Brady's direction.

Brady stilled with shock. *That young man?* Had he misheard? What was wrong with his mother? She hadn't said a word on the walk there.

Emma reached down and checked Betty's leg. There was a large dressing on her shin. Brady couldn't believe he hadn't noticed it before. 'Looking good, Betty. Jim's taking good care of you then.'

Betty beamed.

A one-legged gull hopped to the table near the boy. Betty bent down. Holding a small piece of her ice cream cone she reached towards the bird. Delicately it took the morsel from her hand and gulped it hungrily.

'Wow, how'd you do that? That's so cool. I wish it would take food from my hand.'

'You have to hold your hand very still,' said Betty. Smiling at the boy she repeated the gesture. They were soon lost in their own world, chattering with ease. The gull took food from the boy's hand. 'It's not fair; this bird only has one leg and can't get around like the others.'

'Until he flies. He'll be all right then. You'll see,' said Betty, 'you watch. Fly birdie, fly,' Betty waving at the gull. In a sudden rush of white wings the gull took to the air effortlessly.

'You're right! He did it!' The boy looked down at his own leg.

'Do you have a bad leg too?' asked Betty.

'Yes. I was in a really bad car accident and broke my leg in three places. But I'm getting better. I had a whole leg plaster up to here for two months, and dressings as well. I have a scar. See? Mum says it looks like a half-moon, but I think it looks like lightning.' He turned his leg for Betty to have a better look.

'Definitely lightning,' she responded. The boy smiled and returned to his chips.

Betty leaned in close to the blonde and whispered. Emma shot Brady a look of mild alarm and patted her hand. Betty gripped the woman's arm.

Brady attempted a smile. It must have been a poor effort because the blonde's eyes clouded. Betty's whispering grew more intense.

Brady rose and went over to their table, extending his hand to Emma. 'Hello, I'm...'

Betty burst into tears and threw herself at the woman. 'Make him go away. He's a stranger. He's been following me all day.'

'I don't believe this!' Brady threw his hands heavenward.

'I think you'd better step back, sir,' said Emma. 'I don't know who you are, but you're upsetting my client.'

'Your "client"? Oh, that's rich,' muttered Brady. 'Listen lady...'

Betty clutched at Emma's sleeve. 'Take me home, Emma. *Please.* Jim will be worried. I don't like this man.'

Brady took a step closer and Betty's sobs grew louder. Brady's jaw dropped. Emma rose decisively. Linking her arm through Betty's she beckoned to the boy, who was now also looking worried.

'Oh, for crying out loud,' Brady said, reaching for his wallet. Unbelievable. He would actually have to show this woman his ID. He fumbled with the wallet. 'Wait a minute...ah, Miss...'

'Look, sir. It doesn't really matter right now who you are. Right or wrong, Betty's upset. I am her nurse.' Emma pointed to the badge on her shirt. 'I see her twice a week. The best thing we can do right now is for me to take her home to familiar surroundings. The best thing you can do is step aside and work this out later, okay.'

Before Brady could utter another word, the trio walked quickly across the road to a white hatchback with Noarlunga Community Nursing scripted on the side. 'Bloody hell!' Brady slumped back onto the bench.

An old man sitting nearby dragged himself stiffly out of his chair, then giving Brady a wide berth, shuffled as quickly as he could across the road.

Retrieving his mobile from his pocket, Brady quickly punched in his father's number. He'd have to interrupt Jim's game of golf and tell him to return home. It wouldn't do for his mother to arrive home to an empty house. He'd never hear the end of this. The mobile displayed one bar. Out of service. Thrusting the mobile back into his pocket, he cursed out loud.

Brady was shaken by his mother's reaction. She'd always seemed fine on the phone. What had just happened? Had his mother really not known him?

A tap on his shoulder startled him out of his reverie.

'Excuse me, sir, but I would like you to accompany me to the station to answer a few questions,' said a stern looking policeman.

I didn't know

'Are you Gran's nurse?'

Emma turned from writing in Betty's care plan as a slim young girl entered the room. 'Sorry?'

'I'm Ebony, the granddaughter.' The girl, who looked in her mid-teens slid over the side of the lounge opposite Emma and sat in it sideways. She tilted her head and regarded Emma through eyes as black as her long hair.

'Shit.' Emma dropped her pen. 'Sorry. That just came out.'

The girl giggled.

Emma worried her bottom lip with her teeth. 'Oh dear. I didn't know Jim and Bet...your grandparents had children.'

'Just one. My dad.'

'You're kidding!'

'Who's kidding? Would you like a cup of tea, Emma dear?' Back in familiar surroundings Betty was lady of the manor. Without waiting for an answer she left for the kitchen.

Jim wandered in. 'Emma, hello. It's not your day to visit, is it? No, it's Sunday. Of course. It's lucky we were home. Eb and I were going to play golf but changed our minds.'

'*You* changed *your* mind, Grandie.'

'You look a little pale Emma.' Jim crossed the room.

Betty arrived back in the room wearing a stained apron and carrying a plate of biscuits at a precarious tilt.

'What are you doing Bett? Those biscuits are stale, love.' Jim walked towards her.

Betty swung around to Jim. Several of the biscuits slid off the plate. She burst into tears. 'Don't yell at me Jim.'

'Here Gran, don't worry. I'll clean up.' Ebony put a gentle arm around her grandmother, took the plate and picked up the biscuits.

'I'm a silly old duffer.' Betty flapped her hands.

'I think you might need a nap, Bett. You've had a big morning.' Jim gave Emma a pleading look and steered Betty away. 'It's alright, love.'

'Good idea, Jim.' Emma nodded. 'See you in a minute.'

Ebony wandered into the kitchen and returned with a brush and dustpan. 'I won't get the vacuum out, Gran hates the noise.'

Emma turned to the care plan and flicked through the notes. She wasn't going to find anything; she'd taken Betty's history herself. Next of kin was Jim Harcourt and person to contact was Steve Harcourt. No mention of a son. She scanned the room for family photographs. A wedding photograph of Jim and Betty had pride of place and on the side buffet. Next to it was a photograph of young couple with a small child that she hadn't noticed before.

'What's going on, Emma? Where's my son?' Jim stood beside Ebony's chair and ruffled her hair.

Emma folded her arms. 'The tall hairy guy? The one who looks like a homeless man? *The one you failed to mention*, Jim?'

Jim paled. 'Oh.'

Ebony slid back into the armchair with an amused smile. 'Tut, tut, Grandie, are we a family secret?'

Jim shot her a warning look. 'Ah, Emma. So you met Brady.' He ran a hand over his bald pate.

'I wouldn't exactly say I "met" him. Jim.'

'Was there a problem.'

'You could say that.'

'Jim, I can't find my teeth,' Betty called out.

'Be back in a tick,' said Jim.

'There's something wrong with Gran, isn't there. Other than her leg ulcer, I mean.' Ebony swung one leg absently. She looked around. 'It's okay. Grandie will be a while seeing to Gran.'

Emma sighed and sat down.

'I've noticed a few things, you see. I've been here for a

couple of weeks with Grandie and Gran. Dad had to finish up at work. Did you really not know about us?'

'No. Your Gran has only been a patient for a few weeks. Noarlunga might be a small town, but it's impossible to know everything about a few thousand people.' Emma smiled.

'Prudence Wainwright does.'

'You know her?' Emma laughed. 'You have learned a lot in a short time. You're a smart cookie, Ebony. Do you want a job?'

Ebony screwed up her nose. 'I can't stand the sight of blood.'

'You're observant. I'll give you that. Tell me what you've noticed with your Gran.'

'Well, sometimes it's little things like putting the oven on and forgetting. Or telling you the same thing over and over. But when she's really tired she just stares out of the window and then looks straight through you as if you're not there. The other day she got in the car and didn't know how anything worked. She put the key in and then didn't seem to know what to do next. You know, like she'd never seen any of it before. Then she got a bit upset and said she'd changed her mind. She told Grandie she had a headache and he could do the shopping. I didn't say anything. He doesn't see it. I tried to talk to him about it, but he got a bit upset so I left it. Like, what do I know? I'm fifteen, but I'm just a kid to them. Anyway, we haven't visited for three years, not since Mum died here in an accident.' Ebony sat upright and leaned forward, dark eyes earnest. 'I haven't imagined it, have I?'

'No, you haven't.'

'Grandie will have to see it now. She should've known who Dad was, even with his homeless look.'

'Sometimes it takes a fresh pair of eyes, Ebony.'

'I haven't talked to Dad about it. He only just arrived and we've kinda been fighting. Not important stuff, you know, just ... Oh jeez, he's going to be really pissed off with you bringing Gran home.'

'He'll live.' Jim wandered in.

'Jim, sit down. We need to have a chat.' Emma opened the blue folder and picked up her pen.

Reef café

'The waiting time for an appointment is positively scandalous, Sister Tesler,' said Prudence, 'and the cost! It's getting so that one cannot afford to be ill anymore. Not that I care much for myself mind, Earl does provide well.'

Emma spied her mother, Iris, waiting at their favourite table in the courtyard of the Blue Reef Café. 'I have to meet my...'

Prudence Wainwright didn't miss a beat even though Emma was openly staring at her watch. 'It's the poor old ones I worry about. I mean, how does lovely Jim Harcourt manage with that handful of a wife who's off with the fairies? Why, they seem to be in the medical centre every other day. How are they doing?'

'You know I can't...'

'Of course, dear. I'm not prying. I can't abide gossip. However, one can't help but...'

'I really have to go, Prudence,' said Emma, forgetting the offence the woman took to being called by her given name. Prudence Wainwright only tolerated such familiarity from her equals.

Prudence pulled her handbag further up her arm with an air of blighted indignation. Adjusting her hat firmly on her head, she spun on her highly polished heel and chose a table in the cafe.

'Hi Mum.' Emma slumped into the seat opposite her mother.

'Lucky escape?' laughed Iris, as Emma sat. 'That woman is incorrigible. Who was she "not gossiping" about today? Or dare I ask? You look tired darling, is everything okay?'

'Oh Mum, you won't believe what happened?'

'Let me guess. Jim Harcourt's son. Over the arrest saga?'

Emma spilled her coffee. 'Oh no! How many people know about that?'

'What's the population of Noarlunga?'

'Oh, dear, I should've guessed, and I suppose everybody has their own version of events. There must be dozens of stories.'

'All eyewitnesses,' said Iris, earning a stern look.

'Wasn't I silly to think it would all blow over? I've no idea how the police got involved. I just bustled Betty into the car, which I probably shouldn't have done. But you should have seen her, she was so distressed, calling her son a stranger and said he'd been following her.'

Iris patted her arm. 'Oh darling. I don't know what else

you could have done.'

'Poor Betty. I'm quite concerned. I've noticed her mind wandering when I've been there to do her dressings. I can't believe I didn't know she had a son.'

'Well it's hardly your fault darling if you're not told. Where has this son been?'

'He's been living in Sydney.'

'Ah, that might explain a bit. If he's their only child, Jim and Betty might have felt abandoned, especially if he hasn't been home much.' Iris waved the waitress away. 'Did Betty settle when she got home?'

'Yes. Thank goodness Jim was home from golf. He had his granddaughter with him, pretty thing, hair like midnight. As soon as Betty saw them she was her old self. She seemed to forget that anything happened.'

'Jim was okay then?'

'Thankfully yes, and it gave me a chance to discuss Betty's mental state.'

'Is it Alzheimer's do you think?'

'She'll need assessment. And tests.'

'But this situation!' Emma rested her head on the table. 'What a mess. But honestly Mum, the son looked like a jail escapee, or a homeless person. And attitude! He should be arrested for that if nothing else.'

'Oh my!' giggled Iris. 'I'm sorry, but it is amusing.'

'I doubt Mr Grumpy is anywhere near amused. I guess I should clear the air with him.'

'Good luck with that, darling!'

Emma frowned.

Emma sighed as she watched her mother leave, then ordered an apple juice. She faced a blissful weekend off-duty and after a quick swim she intended to do nothing more energetic than go home and catch up on some reading. She'd worry about apologies and explanations on Monday.

Emma felt a trickle of water down her back.

'Oh Steve! One day you're going to get knocked out cold for that trick!' Emma shrieked.

'Why darling, aren't you pleased to see me?' he purred, shaking his hair, showering Emma as he planted himself in the chair Iris had vacated.

'No, I'm not!' Emma wiped salty drips from her face. 'What are you doing here?'

'Nice to see you too,' Steve's eyes narrowed. 'I hear you've met my nephew.'

'Your nephew?' Emma squeaked.

Steve put his hands behind his head and smiled. 'I have it on excellent authority that you made quite an impression on my nephew, Brady Harcourt.'

'Oh! Crap. He's your *nephew*? Of course he is. I keep forgetting you're Jim Harcourt's brother. Oh dear, I didn't even know Jim and Betty had a son.'

'Why Emma, you're really upset about this.'

'Of course I am. I practically kidnapped Betty from her own son. Who looks like a Yeti, by the way. What is he? Has he been living with gorillas in Borneo? And...stop laughing. I've just been fending off Prudence Wainwright, the town gossip, because she's always pumping me for information and now I feel like an idiot.'

'Never!' grinned Steve.

'I know what I should have done.' Emma sat upright. 'I should've pumped Prudence. I bet if I sat down with her for a few hours she'd fill me in on the whole town. Oh Steve, I thought I was doing the right thing. I thought this debacle couldn't get any worse.'

'Oh, but you're wrong, Emma,' said Steve. 'Haven't you heard? My oh-so-law-abiding nephew was taken in for police questioning.'

Emma's mouth formed an 'O'. She didn't risk speech. If her voice went up another octave she'd just die.

'And you want to know the funniest part?' Steve leaned forward intently. 'He thinks you ratted him out to the cops!'

Afraid

'Does she need stitches?' Ebony leaned forward in the chair, anxious eyes on Emma.

'Let me have a look honey.' Emma sat down, carefully. 'You're Bridget Galloway, aren't you?'

The girl's lank, over-dyed black hair hung in stringy cords around her pale face. She began to tremble. Her eyes glazed.

'Take deep slow breaths, Bridget.' Emma grabbed a coat and put it around the girl's shoulders.

'Is she going to pass out?' Ebony put her arm around Bridget.

'I don't want stitches. I don't want doctors.' Bridget's voice was shrill, afraid. She began to rock slightly, back and forth.

'You don't have to, honey.' Emma patted the girl on the knee and was pleased to see her relax. 'I see someone has given you first aid of a sort.' Emma eyed the bloody wad Bridget was holding against her forehead.

'That was me. I always carry one of Dad's

handkerchiefs,' Ebony pulled on the hem of her school uniform.

'Not a used one I hope.'

'Oh no, I wouldn't do that. Thanks for seeing us.'

'You're lucky I heard the tapping on the back door. Only the staff come in that way and they don't knock.'

'We didn't want anyone to…' Bridget murmured.

'But nosy Mrs Wainwright was in the carpark with another old woman. She saw us, and she's like the worst gossip ever. Is it true Bridge doesn't have to see a doctor? She wouldn't go to the school nurse.'

'That stupid nurse would ring Da.'

'I had to help her through a gap in the fence.'

'So I'm harbouring fugitives. Thanks for relieving the boredom girls.' Emma shook her head and chuckled. 'Honestly though, you don't have to see anyone. No one will force treatment on you. That's not how we work. You always have a choice. Why, Bridget could just hold that hankie on her head for as long as she liked. Of course, it might get stuck there.'

Bridget's eyes widened.

'And you don't have to tell anyone? Even though we're minors?' Ebony asked. 'That's great! I sprained my ankle at school back in Sydney, and our deputy head couldn't wait to get on the phone to Dad. I thought he was going to drive off the Harbour Bridge. He's so overprotective.'

'You're both fifteen. You can get any kind of medical

help you choose. You have a right to confidentiality with treatment. Mind you, schools have different responsibilities, but we won't go there...So, Ms Galloway, are you ready for me to take a look? I assume you didn't come here for the ambience or fascinating conversation.'

Emma worked quickly.

'You alright Bridge? What are those things you're putting on ... Sister?'

'Call me Emma. They're steri-strips, they'll hold the wound together instead of stitches.'

'That's a relief. I thought she'd need yards of stitches. Her head just split open. She bled like a geyser.'

'The scalp's like that.' Emma placed a small skin coloured dressing on the wound. 'What did she hit? Or should I say who?'

Bridget giggled.

'She was trying to ride my bike.'

'At school? Right.' Emma smiled. 'Well Ms Ebony, you did very well for someone who can't stand blood and guts.'

Ebony blushed. 'Oh. That.'

'Let me get you girls a drink. Tea? Coffee?'

'Oh we're right. We wouldn't want to bother you.' Ebony stood.

'Ah, you've heard of my coffee making ability. Shame. But I insist. I want Bridget to have something hot and sweet, for shock. We don't want her passing out on the way home.'

'Shit no. Oh, sorry.' Ebony flopped back in the chair.

Emma slumped in the chair after the girls left. She might not have known that Jim Harcourt had a son, but she knew about the Galloways. There had been several occasions where the community nurses had to attend to Tom Galloway. His care notes mentioned various injuries from falls, but stopped short of calling the man what he was, a mean drunk.

She'd visited him herself. Not that Tom Galloway would remember her, or any of the other nurses who'd ministered to his breaks and cuts. He'd almost severed a finger once, manically chopping wood. His son, Byron had been there then, steering between obligation and resentment. Wearing a suit, he'd looked out of place with the rundown house. 'Do I have to be here?' he'd asked, looking at his watch, a Tag Heuer. 'I've got to get back to work. My sister will be home from school soon. She'll see to the old man.'

The sweet aroma of marijuana had permeated the house, fighting with the odours of stale beer.

'That's what we're for, Byron,' Emma had said, watching him bouncing on his heels.

'Great. Thanks Sister. Those mobile phones won't sell themselves.' He'd shot her a charming smile, a relieved afterthought.

Bridget had looked so afraid, and lost. It was entirely possible that the girl hadn't seen a doctor in years. She was too thin. Her dyed black hair had seemed lifeless next to Ebony's glowing tresses. The Galloway house had been neat and clean for the most part. That was something.

Emma tidied her desk. It was time to leave. The polyclinic would be open til late, but she needed to lock the community nursing offices. She looked out the window. Ebony was alone in the car park, chewing her nails.

Emma slid the window open. 'Ebony, you okay. Want a lift? Where do you live?' Emma glanced at the young girl, who was humming along to the radio.

'Oh, at the back of Grandie and Gran's. Sorry, of course you wouldn't know.'

'You seem to have settled well into school.'

'Well, yeah. I guess. I met Jenna Bragg on the beach before school started. We kinda started hanging out. We're both new, so that helped, we didn't have to try and fit in. And Bridget, well she's an outcast from all the groups. But she's a really nice kid, you know. Pretty shy. It's weird really. I didn't have too many friends at my last school. I mean, I didn't see much of them out of school.'

'You're liking it here, then.'

'Crap. My bike! I left it at school. Duh!' Ebony thumped her head. 'Ah, doesn't matter, Dad'll drop me off tomorrow.'

'He won't be mad.'

'Nah, he's a pussy cat. He's allergic to conflict.'

'Could've fooled me.'

Ebony giggled.

'Just out of interest, Ebony. How were you planning to get home if I hadn't seen you?'

'Well I wasn't going to walk that far. Bridget walks kilometres—she legged it as soon as we got out the door. She had to get tea at home.'

'You're a bit transparent Ebony Harcourt. You're an odd kid.'

'Thanks, you're a bit weird yourself, especially for an adult.'

'What do you mean "for an adult", you cheeky brat?'

'You say what you think.'

'It's a curse I fight every day.' Emma moaned theatrically. She stopped at the entrance to the street. She didn't want to risk running into Brady. 'You can walk from here, can't you?'

'You could drop me at the door. Dad might not be home.' Ebony paused in the half open car door, eyes pleading.

'Bite me!' said Emma.

Not fishing

The clack-clack of Betty's knitting needles punctuated the silence. Jim looked up from fossicking in his fishing box. Betty smiled warmly at him. All was well in her world; for now. The comfort of their Sunday rituals seemed to be having the desired effect.

Jim stared at the ball of wool zigzagging around the legs of the coffee table in front of Betty. He'd have to remind her to start a new ball soon. If he didn't, she would run out of yarn and become distressed, because she couldn't remember what to do next.

He had to face it. His wife was drifting away from reality. It had been happening for a while. He'd been placating, covering for her. He still put notes out for the milkman even though they hadn't had one for years. The roses had to be pruned on the first day of autumn, no sooner, no later. Jim would have liked to do without the rose bushes, but they were the last reminder of the farm in the Barossa Valley, and Betty loved them.

The newspaper had to be collected every Saturday at 8

am. And worst of all, Jim had to clean his fishing gear every Sunday evening, even though his beloved sport was almost a thing of the past. Betty might forget her way back from the letterbox, but she noticed these small things and became anxious if they weren't done.

It was time to listen to Emma. 'There are medications that might help her, Jim,' she'd said. 'You could take her to a specialist. She needs assessment and tests. She should have known your son, you know that. There are things you can do. A companion dog might help.'

'I'll think about it,' he'd promised. And he would, just not yet. It was definitely worth considering getting a companion dog, especially if it helped Betty to be calmer and connect. A dog would also alert him. Emma was right, she should have known Brady. He dreaded the day when he too slipped into the past.

Sighing as he sunk into the chair he thought of how his life was on hold. He'd stopped doing many things that had once brought him satisfaction, it was all too much trouble.

'How was fishing? Betty asked. 'Did you catch anything?'

'Oh?' he muttered. 'Yes, I caught a Whiting, but I gave it to Bill.'

Jim continued to clean the tackle box. He hadn't been fishing for years. It was easier to pretend.

'That's a shame. I would have loved a piece of fish for

lunch.'

'Don't worry, Bett, I'll get something out of the freezer.'

'Oh, I wouldn't do that if I were you. You know how fussy Mum is about the kitchen. She's never tolerated men in her kitchen. Says they never clean up. Can't say I blame her.'

Jim's heart sank. That was a first. Talking about her parents. He really should talk things over with Brady. He could wring Brady's neck. The day out with his mother had been a disaster, he hadn't handled that well.

After collecting Brady from the police station and vouching for him, making it clear that he was their son and not some granny-stalking pervert, Jim had driven him home.

During the drive he broached the silence. 'What went wrong, son?'

'I don't want to talk about it.'

'Humph, at least that's something we're good at,' muttered Jim as he parked the car.

'Look, I'm sorry, Dad. I'll...see you later.'

Jim had watched Brady trudge down the rough dirt lane to his cottage, his hands thrust deep into his pockets. It wasn't just the incident with Brady that worried him. Betty had been acting out of character for a while.

Only a week before Betty had made a beeline for Brenda Burnside, the wife of the truck driver who'd hit and killed Scarlett. Jim saw the woman's hands shake as she saw Betty closing in on her. Betty stepped out onto the road without a glance, causing a driver to stop and lean on the horn. Clasping her friend's arm, Brenda had gasped. 'Oh dear. What now?'

Betty had been dressed immaculately in a mauve suit. Jim had been held up by traffic, horrified. They'd never had any contact with the Burnsides although they knew who they were, John did odd jobs and Brenda was a property manager for the local real estate.

'Dear, I'm so sorry about it all,' Betty said when she arrived at the table. 'Please do tell your husband, won't you. Not just from me, from us all. We don't blame him for Scarlett's death, you know.' Betty's gaze was intense, but soft.

With a swift pat on Bren's arm, she was gone—striding off down the street, where Jim finally caught up with her. He turned and gave the two women an apologetic look as he hooked Betty's arm through his.

'Oh God,' Jim overheard Brenda say. 'Do you think she knows what she's saying?'

'I'd put money on it,' said her companion.

'Jim, have you fed the chooks?' asked Betty.

Jim groaned. They hadn't had hens for years. He was saved from answering by a knock at the back door.

His mate Bill, clumping in his gumboots, held out a bucket. It was obvious he'd been fishing. Jim damped down his disappointment.

'Hi Bill. Been fishing, mate?'

'Yeah. Brought you a fish to cook for lunch.'

'Wanna come in?'

'Nah, got m'workin' gear on. Your missus wouldn't thank me for coming inside lookin' and smellin' like a fish market.'

'Thanks, Bill,' said Jim, taking the offered bucket.

'No worries, mate. Maybe we can go fishin' again now the prodigal son's back.'

'A man can dream.'

Bill laughed and turned to go. He took a few steps and turned back. 'You know that trouble with the coppers yesterday?'

'Arrggh. How could I forget!'

'Well, seems old Delaney reported your son to the police, but apparently Emma got the blame.' Bill took off his tattered fishing hat to scratch his bald head.

Jim frowned. 'Oh no, Emma would never do that. She was just diffusing the situation. Could've been a lot worse.'

'Well, your son doesn't know that.'

'Oh crikey, I've had enough misunderstandings for one day.'

'It'll sort itself out. These things always do.'

'Now Bill, you're sounding like my brother Steve.'

'You could take a leaf out of his book, Jim.'

Jim's face creased in a wide smile. 'If I had his carefree life Bill, I'd take the whole blasted book!'

Jim settled Betty down for her afternoon rest, handing her a magazine to read. It was past time to talk to Brady. He wandered down the lane and tapped on the door. Brady ushered him into the kitchen where the Saturday newspaper was strewn across the dining table.

'Sit down, Dad. I'll just put the kettle on.'

'Thanks son. Sounds good.'

'Earl Grey, hot and strong with milk and two sugars, right?'

'Not bad. You remembered how I like my tea.'

Jim watched his son as he prepared the tea and put a plate of biscuits on the table. 'You right there, son?'

'Sure, Dad. Apart from finding that nothing is the way I remembered it in my hometown I'm just peachy. Anyway, sit down and take the load off. Er...how's Mum?'

Jim Harcourt sighed. 'She has good days and bad.'

'Mum didn't know me, Dad. Then, when we sat near the kiosk, she was more comfortable with a kid and that nurse.'

'They're familiar.'

'Ouch,' said Brady. 'I guess I had that coming. I've been gone too long.'

'Forget it, son. I have to face things. Your mother has dementia.' Jim's voice rasped. 'Why hell, son, the day might come when she doesn't know me.'

'Oh Dad. I had no idea.'

Jim blew his nose loudly. 'Didn't have much of an idea myself, son. Emma's been great though, put me in the right direction. It's not going to be easy.'

'What can I do?' asked Brady.

'Well, for starters, I reckon you should just come around. Be casual, you know? She's just as likely to know you next time. Apparently, her memory and recognition will come and go. If you just...well, sit and chat at the table. Ordinary things.' Jim sipped his tea. 'I must say I'm glad you lost the beard.'

'Yeah.' Brady shrugged. 'I'll walk you home, Dad. It might help Mum adjust to me if I'm with you. No time like the present.'

Betty showed no sign of her earlier panic when Brady walked through the door with his father. She seemed rested and greeted him gracefully after wiping her hands on her apron.

'Hello, young man. Are you a friend of my husband's? Do come in and make yourself at home. I'll make you a nice cup of tea. Jim has so few visitors these days. I keep telling him he needs to get out more. He used to do so much, but he's become as housebound as a cripple. Can't seem to get through to him. Men.'

With that, Betty took secateurs out of her large apron pocket and went outside.

'What the...' said Brady.

'She's probably going to cut all the heads off the lavender bushes,' said Jim. 'She's easily distracted, it's part of the condition.'

'You're just going to let her?'

'It's better than the alternative,' said Jim.

'Dare I ask, Dad?'

'She gets restlessness and does the same thing over and over. She'd vacuum all day if I didn't stop her.'

'Crikey.'

Jim shrugged.

'You don't think she'd like to...'

'Don't even go there! Your mother is not vacuuming your house.'

Brady grinned. 'Just trying to help, Dad. Keep her out from under your feet.'

'I'm glad to see you haven't lost your sense of humour.'

'I'm glad to see you can still read my mind.'

'Insolent pup!'

Busy

'Hurry up Sister, I haven't got all day!'

Emma sighed and stacked the patient files on her desk to look through later.

'Have a little patience Clive,' she said, entering the treatment room where Clive Brisley, the local high school principal was waiting to have sutures removed. 'I'm not one of your students.' She unwrapped the dressing pack with deft fingers.

'Sorry, Emma. I'm just so stressed. It's such a busy time. You know, start of the school year.'

'In that case I'm surprised you decided to paint the eaves on your house.' Emma detected a red flush creeping up Clive's neck.

'I was cleaning the gutters,' said Clive defensively.

Emma would bet pounds to peanuts she'd heard him say he was painting the eaves.

After making a few phone calls, Emma was anxious to get on with the day.

Kristy, the receptionist stuck her head around the

door. 'Someone to see you, Emma. He says you know him. Something about being a homeless man?'

A tall loose-limbed man stepped into her office.

'I don't have long,' she said, standing behind her desk. 'You! You look different. Less...'

'...derelict?'

'You've lost the beard, well most of it. Going for the metrosexual look?'

'I wouldn't want to be arrested.'

'You weren't arrested.'

He shrugged.

'Nice suit,' said Emma, giving him a sweeping look from head to toe.

'Thanks. I have some job interviews.'

'I wish you luck. You might be able to upgrade your cardboard box.'

'What? Ah, of course, homeless. Touché.'

'What can I help you with?' Emma picked up a pile of papers and tapped them on the table, briskly squaring them off.

'Dad said you had some papers.'

'Yes, I'll drop them off.'

'Good. I'll be home tonight.'

'I didn't mean...'

'Ta ta then, see you later, after work? You know where I live, where you dropped my daughter off the other day. You should start a people retrieval service.' Brady headed for the door.

Emma looked at her paperweight. He wasn't worth it.

Thrusting notes in her satchel, she strode quickly to the back door of the medical centre. Sinking into the seat of her car Emma checked her client list for the morning. There were only three clients. She'd managed to delegate the afternoon list. It was still an inconvenience. Not only would she have paperwork to catch up at the polyclinic, but she'd have a busy morning with clients she knew little about.

Emma arrived at 43 Pleasant Avenue for her first client and moaned. The street name was crooked, and the house looked as if it should be condemned. It had been painted a nauseating yellow half a century ago, and whatever window frames once graced the house's exterior were long gone. She parked outside.

Mr Daley was a new patient, just released from the local hospital after a prolonged stay. The nursing notes on her Patient List Sheet were patchy, 'Frail Aged' didn't give much information. She groaned. If only he'd been assessed before discharge. Well, it shouldn't take too long; she only had to bath and dress him, then check his blood sugar levels and his Webster medication packs.

The interior lived up to the promise of the exterior; it was a living breathing disaster area. A large woman sitting in an ancient armchair beckoned Emma inside. She didn't get up or exert herself to open the door.

Emma pushed the sliding door aside. It gave an unwelcome screech.

"E's in there,' said the woman, pointing to a partly obscured doorway. 'Waiting for 'is bath 'e is. Hates to be kep' waitin'—patience of a flea.'

'That's b'cause it's all a man 'as left to do in life,' bellowed a distant voice.

Emma quickly surveyed the living room, although this was a poor description because it was more like a maze. Piles of women's magazines were stacked in three feet high columns that looked more than a shade precarious. The rest of the room was furnished with random lounge chairs that had seen a few decades of wear and tear, and were also piled up with a variety of bric-a-brac.

'Git a move on. I aint got all day,' said the voice. 'Oh, bloody hell, I 'ave got all day, aint I? A man'd be better off dead.'

'Yeah, well. Shuffle off then, ya miserable git,' muttered a tall lanky man in his early twenties as he flew past Emma. When he reached the haven of the patio, which resembled a corner of the local tip, he lit up a smoke and read the newspaper.

'Did y'put 20 bucks on No Hoper?' laughed the raspy voice from the bedroom. This speech brought on an attack of wheezing reminiscent of some old codger out of a Dickens' novel.

'Oh ullo, y'here at last,' he said, when Emma came into

the room. 'Not another bloody new one.'

'Now Pa. Be nice to the nurse. We can't have them refusing to come, *again*, y'know,' said his wife. She briefly looked up from her magazine. ''e uses the commode first, dear.'

Bert Daley possessed a beak of a nose that dominated his face, perhaps because his face was gaunt and his frame skeletal.

'Crikey! Will y'look at the size of this one! Could fit 'er in y'pocket. How y'gonna lift me around, sweetheart? Did y'bring a crane?' This statement was followed by another wheezing session that clearly exhausted him as much as it amused him.

''E's got newmoaniah,' said his wife knowledgeably. ''Avin' an 'ell of a time, 'e is, poor love.'

'I c'n speak f'meself woman!' yelled Bert.

'Yer don' 'ave t'yell. Y've got blooming good lungs for a man with emphyseemiah.' She sat back, satisfied she'd explained the medical realities. 'is chart's over there, love,' she said, pointing to a corner of the room that couldn't possibly have been accessed in the last decade. 'But I c'n tell yer what t'do. I looked after 'im m'self 'til m'knees give out.'

Emma sighed. There was no way she could get to the dusty table, much less sort through the mess to find his care plan notes, *if* they existed, which she was beginning to doubt.

'C'n y'get me another beer when yer go to the fridge, Mum?' called the youth, looking up from his paper.

'Say *please* t'yer mother, yer waste o' space. And get yer own goddamned beer y'lazy clod. And don't touch mine, yer good f'nothing sloth!'

'Whadya want on the fifth race, Dad?'

'Stuffed if I know. If a man 'ad a chance to look at 'is own paper 'e might be able to tell yer.'

Emma bathed and dried the old man, put him in clean pyjamas and sat him on the armchair in the bedroom. She deftly threw clean sheets on the bed while he wheezed in the corner on a faded armchair, still slyly regarding her with a watchful eye.

Luckily the Daleys were not like her tyrannical ward sisters of the past, because Emma dispensed with every rule of bed-making.

When he was settled back in bed, Bert's sullen-faced son brought him a beer and the paper.

'Great breakfast, Sis! Whadya reckon?' Bert slanted a glance in Emma's direction as he downed the beer straight from the stubby bottle.

'Well, Bert. I reckon I'll have to up your insulin dose.'

He hooted a wheezing laugh.

'You'll do,' he chortled.

In the car, Emma scribbled hurried notes on the back of a work pad. It was a pain not being able to find the care plan.

She would have to chase that up. The community nursing agency would be much easier if it was separate from the polyclinic.

Unexpected

Emma rang the doorbell. She'd come straight from the long day's work to see him. She still wore her uniform and ID badge. Her hair was coiled professionally and pinned up, or it had been that morning. Several stray strands fell errantly over her face. If she had thought about it, she might have tidied up. On the other hand, if she had thought about it, she might not have come at all. But she had agreed to drop off some information sheets on services for dementia sufferers for Brady to look over with his father.

The door flew open and a tall blonde teen smiled down at her. 'Oh, hello,' said the girl. 'I'm Jenna. Jack Bragg's daughter. Come in. Brady's in the kitchen getting in our way.' She raced down the hallway to the back of the house, clearly expecting Emma to follow.

Brady was close on Jenna's heels. Emma was surprised to see him in board shorts and a bright T shirt. 'Do come in Sister Tesler,' he said, throwing the door open and stepping aside.

The kitchen was a hive of activity. The huge oak dining table was strewn with bags of flour, porcelain mixing bowls and a variety of ingredients. Brady ran a finger around the bowl.

'Leave that alone Dad! I'm cooking tonight. Hi Emma,' Ebony waved a wooden spoon at her father.

'You've met?' asked Brady.

'Duh! I told you Dad. I was at Nan and Grandie's when Emma brought Nan home.' Ebony winked at Emma.

'You and a thousand others, I imagine.'

'Yes Dad, you're quite famous. I expect to see you on the front page tomorrow.' Ebony grinned.

'You'll keep.' Brady shrunk into a corner of the kitchen.

'Sorry if this is a bad time,' murmured Emma. 'You have a houseful.'

'Oh, no,' he said, 'I'm just about to be thrown out of my own kitchen anyway.'

Ebony smiled at Emma. 'Don't mind Dad. He's just holding Custer's Last Stand. He swears he can cook pancakes, but we've just thrown one batch out.'

Brady opened the back door and gestured to a bench seat on the patio. 'Don't ask me how I managed to acquire such an, um, interesting menagerie in only a few short weeks.'

'Oh Dad, you didn't acquire anyone. You've hardly been out of the house.' Ebony pushed her father towards the door, eyeing the sheaf of papers in Emma's hand. 'Don't you have things to talk about?'

With a hand under Emma's arm, he guided her towards the door leading to the back patio. Then with an extravagant bow to the girls he said, 'I know when I'm not wanted.'

He sat at one end of the porch swing, while Emma positioned herself at the other. He stretched his legs. 'The gypsy child, Bridget is very sweet and polite, which is more than I can say for my own daughter. And as for Jenna, she's a cross between Sarah Bernhardt and Hitler.'

'You don't seem to be suffering too much.'

Brady shrugged.

'So, how was your day?' Brady leaned an arm along the swing.

'Small talk. Wonderful. I do so love small talk. Sure you don't want to start with the weather?'

'Great for this time of year, isn't it?'

Emma glared at him. 'Surprised you noticed.'

'I grew up around here.' Brady pressed a heel on the timber decking and set the swing in motion. 'I don't want to fight with you. I'm having a really good day. And look at that view. The ocean is darker here than in Sydney. I missed that.'

'How long did you live there?' Emma placed the sheets on the seat beside her.

'Nearly twenty years.' He laughed, a hollow sound. 'I

was only going for a gap year, a mix of surf and part-time volunteering.'

Twilight was creeping from the wide horizon, a pale shroud of mist softened the day's end. The chatter from the girls in the kitchen was accompanied by the buttery sweet aroma of cooking.

'You'd better show me those before it's too dark to see,' he said suddenly. 'And you've probably had a long day.'

'Yes. It's been a shocker.'

'Yes. I've had Steptoe and Son, Don Juan. And you.'

Brady's eyebrows flew up. 'You're very ... candid.'

There was silence for a time.

'I'm sorry I was a jerk.' Brady turned to Emma.

She raised shocked eyes. 'Thank you. You know, you're quite bearable when you're being human.' Emma picked up the papers. 'When you're not the guy with a chip on his shoulder.'

'I wasn't always.'

'I'll take your word for it, for now.' She held his gaze. 'I didn't call the police.'

'I know. Dad's friend Bill told me.'

'So you were just going to let me suffer!'

'Of course,' he said, arms folded.

'You...you! Words fail me.'

'Bet that's rare.'

'Now you're being sarcastic for no good reason.'

'Astute of you. Now, by the way, did you make up a

nickname for me by any chance?'

'Er...as a matter of fact I did. MG.'

'Oh, a sleek, sporty moniker.'

'No. Misery Guts.'

'Oh, you are going to be so sorry you told me that.'

'Really?'

'Yes, I just landed the job as Office Administrator for the Noarlunga Polyclinic.'

Emma's jaw dropped. 'My clinic and...'

'Yes, Sister Tesler. I'm your new...'

'Hey Emma!' Ebony called from the kitchen window behind them. Three faces appeared.

Emma turned quickly, setting the swing rocking. She saw three smiling faces framed by the window. 'What are you three up to?' She laughed.

'...boss.' Brady groaned as the papers hit the floor.

'Come and be our taste tester.' Ebony waved a floury hand.

'Isn't that the job they give the court jester who gets poisoned? I don't trust you lot.' Emma shrugged at Brady, stepped over the papers, and went inside.

The polyclinic

'Chaos alert,' said Kristy, handing Emma a coffee.

'What?' Emma flopped into a chair in the polyclinic staff room.

'Haven't you heard, Emma? Rumblings from above.' Kristy pointed to the ceiling. 'The new boss has called a meeting.'

Emma froze. After Brady's declaration that he was her new boss she'd been playing down the news in her head. There were so many departments in the clinic and the admin were referred to as "the upstairs lot". Even though they'd formed a truce of sorts, the news of his new role had rattled her. And he'd waited for just the right moment to tell her, after she'd been rambling on about work.

'Why? The polyclinic is run by a committee with a board of members, and it's government funded.'

'Melanie's been sacked.'

'What? Melanie Parsons? One of my nurses! Without me knowing—that's a bit high-handed.'

'Oh, come on Emma, you've been complaining about

her for months. She's a lazy loudmouth.'

'Yes, but...'

'We've only got five minutes until the meeting, so I'd spend it drinking that coffee if I were you,' said Kristy.

'What's the deal?'

'I don't know anything. Melanie came in sobbing to collect stuff from her locker. The clinic's lawyer, you know, Eric Wainwright, one of the local councillors, plus the new guy who's just been appointed as director, Harcourt or something, they were with her.'

'What...'

It was pointless. Kristy was gone.

'I'm sorry to do this on your first day on the job, Brady,' said Eric Wainwright.

'It can't be helped,' said Brady.

'If you could just give me a few moments in the spare office, I'll put some thoughts on paper. I'll have to take Sister Tesler aside and ask a few questions. But I won't do it in front of the group. She's a professional, but she will be blindsided by such an action taken without her knowledge. However, time was of the essence. I'll need you there for that. You have no objections?'

'Not at all. Do you need anything?'

'No, I've brought everything,' Eric said, delving into his briefcase for a large yellow legal pad.

Brady withdrew to his own office. He really didn't

need this on his first day. It would take some effort to make sure the day's events didn't put him wrong-footed with the staff. Not how he would have liked to begin his new position.

He slumped into the streamlined leather chair. Why did this debacle have to centre on Emma? Sleep had eluded him the past few nights. That was nothing new, but thoughts of Emma were a new factor. It was both disconcerting and pleasant. He was surprised how hard it was to push her from his mind at odd times during the day. His anger had vanished when he saw her beaming smile to the girls and natural manner with them. And she'd refused to rise to his baiting.

'Ready?' Eric paused at the door. Brady rose and followed him.

Emma threw the coffee in the sink and headed upstairs. With relief, she saw that Jean Blake, the retiring director was chairing the meeting and there was no sign of Brady. The room filled with staff from the various departments; the dental clinic staff, the cardiac intervention sister and the welfare officer. They greeted Jean warmly and chatted to each other. Apparently, nothing in their world had shifted.

Emma's relief vanished when Eric Wainwright entered the room, followed by Brady. Both men wore dark suits and grim expressions. Emma saw some of the girls appraising Brady with open admiration. His hair was slick and shiny. Now, clean shaven and with an indefinable air of control he was the epitome of confident professionalism. She swallowed hard.

Jean got straight to the point. 'Morning all,' she said, 'this is a special meeting for two reasons. As you know, I will be leaving in a week, so today I want to introduce Brady Harcourt, your new director...'

Emma felt dizzy. Jean's words began to run into each other. Why hadn't she been consulted about the sacking of one of her staff? It was unprecedented. She took deep breaths. The room felt airless. She should've had the coffee Kristy offered. Her attention was drawn back to the front as Eric Wainwright stood.

'This is the unpleasant part, so I'll get right down to it,' he said. 'Melanie Parsons was sacked last night.' The room began to buzz. 'Quiet please,' he said, holding up a hand. A distinguished man renowned for his calm persistence, he was instantly heeded. 'Nurse Parsons was responsible for a breach of patient confidentiality that may have contributed to the attempted suicide of one of the teenage clients. This situation called for immediate and direct action.' He turned to look at Emma. 'Sister Tesler, I apologise for appearing to go over your head, but there was no other choice but instant dismissal.'

Emma nodded as Eric continued.

'There will be an investigation. I have extended our sincere regret to the girl's parents and as the clinic's lawyer

I ask for your complete co-operation. This matter will only be discussed in this clinic with the relevant staff, and I ask for the other departments to remain detached from the situation. We do not anticipate media involvement, and there will be no police involvement.'

Eric paused while the news sank in. 'Now, let's put that aside, ladies and gentlemen. I would like to welcome Brady Harcourt, and also to thank Jean Blake for all her years of fine service. She will be here for the next week, but I hope you will all support Mr Harcourt settle in, and assist Jean to skive off as much as possible so she can pack for her...what is it, Jean—your third honeymoon?'

Jean laughed. Eric's secretary arrived with a large cake and the room hummed with conversation and laughter.

To Emma's surprise, Brady mingled effortlessly with the staff.

Eric found his way to her side. 'Please don't worry too much, Emma. I'll be in touch in a day or two and we can have a chat.'

'I look forward to that, Eric. I can see that this is being handled well, but I'm anxious and I'd like answers.'

'Naturally.' Eric smiled.

At any other time, Emma would have enjoyed the party atmosphere, but she couldn't help wondering which one of the troubled teens had attempted suicide. Her heart clenched when she thought of Bridget. She seemed to be getting along well with Jenna and Ebony, but she was vulnerable. Praying that it wasn't the frail dark-haired girl kept Emma from entering the enjoyment.

Surprised

Brady was shocked in wakefulness by a trickle of cold water down his face. 'Fair go, Steve! Don't you ever get tired of teenage pranks?'

'No. Don't you know they call me Peter Pan around town? Get moving buddy, I need your help.'

'How'd you get in? You sure you didn't do time for break and enter? You should.'

'Oh, poor Mister Grumpy. Late night? You look like shit.'

'Gee thanks. I didn't sleep much.'

'If you came surfing with me in the mornings you'd sleep like a baby.'

Brady's eyes showed alarm. 'If you think I'm having one more surfing lesson from you, you've got another thing coming. Nearly didn't survive the last one.'

'You were a kid. I was trying to make you man up. Anyway, get up. Rotary is having a beach concert and you're helping.'

Brady nursed a coffee at the kiosk while Steve opened up his surf shop. Brady stretched his legs, savouring the moment. In spite of the cold and wet early morning start; he felt good, really good. He watched the other patrons. Nearly every table was full. The tables were dotted in a line along the grass, giving each an untarnished view of the beach.

Brady and Steve spent the next few hours in a whirlwind of preparations. Steve's shop had been cleared of most of its contents. There were several wannabe surfers who seemed to view Steve as some kind of demigod. They were slave-like in their devotion to helping. They'd lined the beachfront with a colourful surfboard barrier, and were setting up the porch of the shack with lighting and equipment. By mid-morning Steve declared a break, threw a few chairs around his office, picked up the phone and gave a series of rapid-fire instructions to the local pizzeria.

'Who are you feeding? The five thousand?' asked Brady.

'You, my dear nephew, have been gone too long—and I don't just mean geographically. We're having a quick meeting about the concert.'

Any conversation on the matter was stalled by the arrival of several men who greeted Steve with back-slapping good humour, demanding he empty the beer fridge. With the ease of long acquaintance Steve placed a drink in front of each man.

'Memory like an elephant,' said a burly man, 'never forgets a man's poison.'

Steve placed a can of lemonade in front of Brady and was rewarded with a filthy look. Brady grabbed the beer out of his hand. Steve laughed and got another, then introduced Brady to the men.

The burly man was Jack Bragg, a private detective, and Jenna's father.

'Quite a shock she gave me, my Jenna,' said Jack. 'She was supposed to come for the holidays. What I didn't realise was that she was here to stay. Said there was a letter on its way; she couldn't imagine how we'd missed it. Sly puss. Sometimes she forgets she has a private detective for a father. That naive nonsense might work on her mother, but not me.' Jack roared laughing.

'You don't mind then?'

'Mind? No, I'm thrilled. Our two girls seem to have hit it off, so it's good to meet you. Your girl has serenity, perfect foil for my firecracker. Not sure about the other girl though, Bridget, bad background there I think.'

'She's shy, but polite. Helpful kid. Has the Goth thing going on, but she seems a bit half-hearted about it if you ask me.'

'How's Jim doing?' asked Jack.

'He's probably staying home with Mum. She doesn't cope well with crowds anymore.'

The beach was soon crowded and a local rock band, the Redbacks, started playing. Steve was buzzing back and forth, everywhere at once. Brady took one of the deckchairs from Steve's shop and sat on the beach. He tied a handkerchief and put it on his head. He should have nicked one of the caps from the shop. He used to have beach gear. Probably still did somewhere.

Brady's phoned beeped. As he bent to pick it up Ebony plonked down beside him, giving him a brief hug. 'Hey, Dad.' Brady's hand jerked on the mobile, cutting the caller off.

'Damn,' said Brady.

'Is that any way to greet your only child?' said Ebony. 'Jeez Dad, what's with the handkerchief. You look like an old fart.'

'It's hot. How much do you want?'

'Only 30 bucks.'

'I thought the concert was free.'

'It is, but a girl has to eat, Dad. Honestly. Anyway, I thought you wanted to connect with me.'

'Not through my wallet, I don't.'

He handed over the notes and was rewarded by a peck on the cheek.

'Keep the rest, buy yourself a hat. You know I love you, Dad.'

'Ever heard of 'cupboard love', Eb?'

'Sure Dad, you know I'm in lurve with my cupboard.'

'Bah!'

Ebony ran and linked arms with Jenna.

Brady looked at his mobile screen. Julia Prescott; the deputy principal at Ebony's Sydney grammar school. 'On my way xxx.'

He vaguely remembered a casual invitation to call in if she was ever in Adelaide. Or had it been at her instigation? It was hard to tell with Julia.

Back in Sydney they'd shared a few casual meals. Julia would be expecting a fancy restaurant, but it wasn't possible to flit off to a trendy suburb. A beach rock concert would not go down well.

Cursing himself for a fool, Brady retrieved her number.

'I'm driving darling, can't it wait?' Julia turned the radio down.

'Can you park on the side of the road?'

'Not really. I'm on the Southern Expressway, I don't want to miss the exit. Why? Are you pulling out on me?'

Brady could picture the pout. 'No, I just wanted you to know we're going to a beach concert, that's all.'

'*A what!*'

Smash! The shiny red mobile phone hit the car window, flung there by its owner. Julia Prescott swore. Loudly.

For the first time since meeting Brady, Julia wondered if she was making a monumental fool of herself.

While playing a careful waiting game with the grieving widower it hadn't occurred to her that she might lose. Julia Prescott never lost.

Intrusion

'*I want to rock and roll all night and party every day.*'
Music blared across the beach as the evening revellers
jived to the beat of the KISS hit song. The food stalls had
been dismantled and the beach had been taken over by
families with blankets. Close to the temporary stage, the
younger crowd was dancing.

Ebony was mystified. Why hadn't her father told her
he'd invited her old school Deputy Head to visit? Ms
Prescott wore a jade satin dress that fitted like a glove.
She'd been quite a sight picking her way across the beach
in high heels. This shining vision was not the Ms Prescott
Ebony remembered. She hadn't felt one way or the other
about her at school, but seeing the woman glued to her
father, with her false tinkling laughter was *so
unappealing.*

'Just call me Julia, sweetie,' Miss Prescott said,
wrapping herself around Ebony like a long-lost best
friend.

In a pig's eye, thought Ebony, forcing a smile as she left to find Jenna.

'What's up with you, Eb?' said Jenna.

'Look! At her!

'Who her?' Jenna turned, and stared. 'Wow, is that a model or something?'

'No, it's my old Deputy Principal.'

Jenna whistled. 'She doesn't look old.'

'Don't you get it?' Ebony hissed. 'Dad's supposed to be connecting with me, not some tarted-up version of God-knows-what.'

'Jeez Eb, don't you want your dad to have a life.'

'It's not that. Look at her. She's acting weird, all fake. She's like a leech. I have to keep them apart. Think of something Jenna. God, I'll just die if they start making out. I didn't know they'd even met out of school stuff, but the way they're acting, there must have been a lot more going on.'

'Not overreacting, are we?'

Emma pouted. 'I want Dad to have, well, real love. You know, when two people fit.'

'And you've decided this one doesn't fit. Who would fit your dad, Ebony?'

'I dunno. Someone like Emma.'

'Don't you know what a disaster it is to match people up?'

'Oh, shut up!'

'Okay!' Jenna shrugged and walked away, then

returned with Jack and Helena, who began chatting to Brady and Julia.

Jenna put an arm around Ebony's neck. 'Hey Eb. Have you danced yet?'

Ebony frowned at Jenna.

'No, she hasn't,' said Brady.

Ebony scowled. Thanks Dad, treat me like I'm invisible, then throw me to the lions. She shot Jenna a poisonous look, but Jenna ignored her, dragging her into the middle of the dancing throng.

'You're supposed to be helping me get those two apart. With a crowbar if necessary!' hissed Ebony, then hiccupped. 'Oh damn.' She hiccupped again.

'Dance, you spaz,' said Jenna. 'Don't worry. It's all part of my master plan.'

'Some frigging plan. Introduce Miss Tart to the locals so she feels even more at home. Good one, Jenna.'

Jenna just smiled, tapped the side of her nose slyly and jived her heart out. Ebony opened her mouth to protest, but merely hiccupped, loudly.

'Hold your breath,' said Jenna.

'I beg – hic – your pardon?'

'It'll help get rid of your hiccups.'

'Really Einstein – hic – don't you think – hic – that I've been – hic – told that like – hic – a thousand times.'

'You need to shut up to hold your breath, Eb.'

Ebony rolled her eyes. Then, she did stop breathing.

Coming towards them was the most beautiful boy, make that human being, she'd ever seen. The vision stopped when he came to the two girls.

'Aren't you going to introduce me to your gorgeous friend, Jenna?' he said.

'Oh you! Haven't you got anything better to do than torment me?' said Jenna. 'Oh, all right. Ebony, this is Helena's son, my step-brother, and general nuisance, Antonio. He's working with my dad for a while.'

'Oh,' said Ebony.

'Hey Eb,' said Jenna, 'Your hiccups are gone.'

'You had hiccups? Ah. Hold your breath,' said Antonio.

'I think she just did,' said Jenna, winking and moving aside to allow Antonio into the circle.

'Hi,' he said, 'I'm Antonio.'

'Don't listen to him. We call him Ants,' said Jenna.

'Untrue, only the cruellest of tormenters call me that, of which I am pleased to say there is only one.' Antonio looked straight at Jenna. She poked her tongue out at him.

Ebony laughed. Looking over her shoulder she noticed her father was dancing with Helena, and Jack was spinning Miss Tart around. The sour look on the lush redhead's face was all the satisfaction Ebony needed. 'Very good, Jenna. Sorry I doubted you,' Ebony whispered.

The heavens opened and rain bucketed down. It was one of those sudden Australian summer storms that came with no warning at the end of a humid day. A loud crack of thunder heralded the storm's intention.

Children squealed with delight and twirled; older ones thinking of home jumped to their feet, folded their deckchairs and headed for their cars.

Only the band was shielded by the long colourful awning over Steve's store veranda. Without missing a beat, they played on as the teen element gathered nearer, gleefully enjoying the cool change and the relief of the rain.

Their joy was short-lived. The band started to pack up at the end of the song.

Steve bolted to the stage where he collided with Brady. Then they worked together systematically to clear the stage and stow the banners and equipment in Steve's store.

Steve threw a few towels at Brady. 'Here. Take these. Get a move on, you're soaked through.'

'Where are the girls?' asked Brady.

'Depends which ones you mean,' said Steve. 'Ebony and Jenna sloped off with that handsome Spanish boy.'

'What! Why didn't you tell me before?'

'Don't worry, Junior. Antonio is Helena's kid. He'll take them to Jack and Helena's—*safely.*' Steve crossed his arms, smirking. 'And the fancy redhead went in the opposite direction. Reckon she'd be halfway to the airport to catch a flight back to Sydney by now.'

'Crap,' said Brady. 'I forgot about her.'

Crossed

Eric Wainwright and Brady were waiting outside Emma's office when she arrived at work.

'I'm sorry you've had to wait a few days, Emma, but it was unavoidable.' With a quick nod to Brady and a gentle guiding hand in the small of her back, Eric walked to her office.

'Please, take a seat gentlemen.'

Both men sat while Eric took some papers from his briefcase. Emma could see why Eric was highly regarded, he exuded quiet dignity. How had he ended up with Prudence, the town gossip?

'How have you found Nurse Parsons?' he asked.

'I have had problems with her that I've carefully documented. She overrides patient autonomy and is unprofessional.'

'Have you referred these concerns on?'

'Yes, I have. But I don't want to put the blame on Jean.'

'Don't worry, Sister. We need to deal with the fallout and work out ways to prevent this happening in the future.'

'I need to know who has been compromised,' said Emma.

'Tiffany Belmore,' said Eric. 'News of an abortion was overheard and passed on to the girl's parents. They reacted; badly I'm afraid. We believe the fallout triggered the girl's suicide attempt. Regrettable all round.'

'We don't have a client of that name in community nursing. She must have seen a doctor in the after-hours clinic. In that case, this is an issue for the after-hours medical centre staff,' said Emma. 'However, sometimes the community nurses step in when the clinic is short staffed. This crossover with the GP service is problematic.'

'Thank you, Sister, you've been most helpful,' said Eric. 'I gather from this that you don't know the girl involved.'

'No, I don't. I can only assume that Nurse Parsons filled in at the clinic and obtained the information that way. Her loose talk is most worrying. How did the parents find out about the girl's abortion?'

'We believe Nurse Parsons was overheard at a nightclub. We will get to the bottom of this.'

'That's inexcusable. The girl is a primary concern.' Emma tapped the desk with her pen. 'I do have one suggestion if I may.'

'Please. Go on,' said Eric.

'I'm assuming the girl was admitted to the local hospital after the suicide attempt. Perhaps an immediate transfer to a specialist mental health ward in one of the city hospitals can be arranged. Hospital gossip is hard to control and would only compound the problem. There are excellent mental health teams that organise follow ups.'

Eric turned to Brady. 'Check into that, will you Brady.' He stood and shook Emma's hand.

Brady saw Eric to the door and then returned to sit across from Emma. 'I'm sorry about all this Emma.'

'How old is the girl, Brady?'

'Sixteen.'

'Then she's entitled to confidentiality. The parents should know that.'

'Not everyone would agree with you on that.'

'It doesn't matter,' said Emma, 'in the eyes of the law Tiffany has the right to treatment without parental consent. Any treatment.'

'So you wouldn't have encouraged her to tell her parents?'

'Of course I would.' Emma bristled. 'But ultimately, it's the girl's choice.'

'You're not a parent.'

'You're not a frightened young female.'

'I'm sorry. We're off on the wrong foot again.'

'Suit yourself. It's your foot.' Emma reached into her top drawer.

'What are you doing?' asked Brady.

'Getting a lolly to stop me from biting my tongue.' Emma said sweetly. 'Would you like one?'

'Is it an olive branch?'

Emma glared. 'No, it's a frigging Butter Menthol.'

'Ah. Then let me offer you an olive branch. Dinner?'

'Oh, I couldn't take any more pancakes. They were half-baked, like your...'

'I thought we called a truce.' Brady grinned.

'When it comes to you and me, a treaty document would be more appropriate.'

'I want that in writing.'

'I'll call a committee. My people will get back to your people.'

'Tonight then? 7 o'clock okay?'

'No, it's not. I'm not going on a date...'

'Doesn't have to be a date. A meeting for improvement of staff relations. Oh come on, have pity on a guy. It would really help me out with the job. 6 pm then? What do you say?'

'I think it might be against policy, Mr Harcourt. You are, as you so clearly stated, my boss.'

'I'm not really. The committee is. I was just...'

'Why should I?' Emma's stomach rumbled.

'Hunger?'

Emma threw the Butter Menthol at him.

Brady caught it deftly, tore the paper off and slipped it into this mouth as he left the room.

Emma kicked the rubbish bin.

Brady poked his head through the door five minutes later with an extra-large coffee and a huge chocolate macadamia cookie, clearly gourmet fare from the café across the road.

'Oh heaven,' sighed Emma, then made a serious attempt to frown.

'Why thank you, Sister Tesler. I've never been called heaven before.'

Emma groaned.

Brady smiled. 'It'll keep you going until tonight.'

'All right. 6 o'clock. But I choose, straight after work. Benito's, the pizzeria opposite the hairdresser's. And I'll meet you there.'

Not a date

'It's not a date, Steve. It's work. I'm going straight...there. I should have left already.' Brady wondered if Steve was adopted. He was so unlike his brother Jim, Brady's father. 'Don't make me wish I'd asked someone else to stay with Eb.'

'Ah, but where else could you find someone who would lie to your daughter that you have a work meeting.'

'It *is* a work meeting.'

'Whatever you say,' said Steve. 'Where was I? Oh yes...and pretend I need to use my nephew's computer because the internet is mucking up at my cabin, when my service is actually far superior.'

'Now, that is a deception I'm thankful for,' said Brady. 'Ebony thinks she's old enough to stay home alone.'

'She is. Jim's next door, for heaven's sake. And even if he wasn't.'

'Dad has Mum to worry about.'

'Pray tell, how many of the staff will be attending this professional soirée?'

'Hundreds,' said Brady, pushing Steve towards the bedroom door. 'Don't you have to *use the internet*?'

'Pants on fire.'

'Is something on fire, Uncle Steve?' Ebony stood anxiously in the hall.

'No pet, I was just telling your father that I won't be cooking your dinner, so there's no fear of a fire. He was greatly relieved and offered to pay for pizza delivery. Isn't that a hoot?'

'You'll keep,' said Brady.

'Oh, goodie, thanks Dad. I'd kill for pizza.'

'Don't mention it, Bub...Eb. Anything for my girl.'

Ebony chewed on her bottom lip. Stepping forward to take over her father's awkward attempts at fixing his tie, she hesitated. 'Is there something you want to tell me, Dad?'

'Of course not, Eb. Why do you ask?'

'You're only ever this accommodating when you're guilty.'

'Oh, touché, my pet,' said Steve.

'Haven't you found the computer yet, Steve?' Brady scowled.

'I've gone off the idea. You two are much more entertaining. Besides, I'm waiting for cash for the pizza. Why don't you go and order, Eb? I'll have a meat-lover's.'

Ebony ran excitedly to the phone and could be heard ordering two large pizzas.

'*Two large!*' Brady stared into his wallet.

'Shush, Dad. I'll have it cold for lunch.'

'Yeah, shush, Dad,' said Steve, his hand extended.

Brady crushed several notes into Steve's hand. 'Thief!'

'Liar.'

Brushing past Ebony on his way out, Brady pecked her on the cheek. 'Sure you're okay with me going out, Eb?'

'Why wouldn't I be? Honestly Dad, it was only a couple of months ago that you wouldn't have even been home by now. I don't see what all the fuss is about.'

'Yeah Dad! Okay! Enough's enough,' said Steve, raising his hands in mock surrender.

'Go and have a good time,' said Ebony, nudging her father.

'It's a...'

'*Work meeting,*' chimed Ebony and Steve, then high fived each other.

Brady loped to the car. Ebony was right—he was feeling pangs of guilt, especially after his determination to keep a polite working distance from Emma. He resolved to leave early. Extend an olive branch, have a quick meal and make his excuses. And he would never lie to Ebony again. Steve was right. Ebony didn't need minding.

When Brady arrived at the pizzeria, Emma was already there. She was seated by the side door, looking for all the world as if she might bolt at any minute. She was still in her uniform, she intended to keep this meeting on a professional level. He saw a pizza delivery boy head out the door with a large red heating pack, probably bound for his place. He saw Emma check her watch. Maybe this was a mistake, but then she turned and smiled.

Sitting opposite Emma, Brady set out to put her at ease. 'I'm sorry about today. The issues cut close to home for me. I'm the father of a fifteen-year-old girl, and Scarlett was bipolar.'

'It's okay, I have a friend with bipolar.'

'Then you understand better than most.'

The waiter arrived to take their order. Brady deferred to Emma to order her own, then placed his order. 'Would you like to share some garlic bread?' he asked.

'I'd love it,' she said. 'Have you been here before? Benito makes wonderful pizzas.'

'It smells amazing in here,' he said. 'I didn't realise how hungry I was.'

'There's something about great aromas that pique an appetite.'

The garlic bread arrived and they tore it apart. Brady watched Emma lick her fingers in delight. It was something Ebony did too. He'd told her she should grow out of it, but maybe he was wrong.

'Emma, if you don't mind me asking, how does your friend cope? With bipolar, I mean. There were groups in Sydney, but Scarlett wouldn't go.'

'Very well really. I have worried, but she's holding her

own. She's brutally honest about it, that helps. And she has a pact with her doctor to go to him when she's struggling. That seems to take the pressure off her as well as the family. It's a tough gig.'

'I can't imagine that kind of openness.' Brady's eyes clouded.

The waiter arrived with the pizzas.

Brady wiped his hands on a serviette. 'On another note, Emma, I have some news I think will please you. The council has passed a motion to purchase the house near the hospital for the community nursing agency. Your submission was successful.'

'Oh, that's wonderful.'

The next hour passed in a haze as they discussed the details of the new location and operation. Brady realised how much work Emma had put into the planning and proposal. He watched her eyes light up as she attacked her pizza with gusto.

'Do you want dessert?' he asked. 'Coffee?'

'Oh no, thanks. I'll have enough trouble sleeping with the excitement of the news. By the way,' Emma tilted her head, 'does this mean you've set a world record for the shortest boss in history?'

'I'm not short. I thought at 5/11 I would be classified as...'

'Ha Ha.'

'Okay, yes. I will only be your boss for as long as it takes to secure the building and relocate.'

'Ah, good. One day then.'

'Whoa, that's a bit fast. You're not that good.'

'Watch me,' she said, snapping her purse shut. She stood. 'Thanks for the news, and for the pizza.'

'Thanks for asking me.'

'I didn't,' she said. 'I'm going to have to learn not to bite with you aren't I?'

'Oh, I don't know. You could bite me a little,' he said, earning a stern look.

'About the news. May I inform my staff?'

'Certainly.'

'That's everything then.' She moved towards the door.

'I'll sort the bill.' Brady gestured to a passing waiter. 'My shout.'

Emma headed for her car. As she turned the key in the lock she felt a tap on the shoulder. Turning quickly she found Brady inches from her. His eyes were smoky as they dropped lazily to her chest. She blushed. He smiled, a slow secret curve to his lips.

'May I?' he asked with precise politeness. His hand reached towards her. 'I've been dying to do this all evening.'

'What are you doing? This could be workplace harassment.'

'We're in a carpark—of a restaurant, of your choosing.'

'That's no excuse. It's...'

The carwash across the street started up, drowning out the rest of her sentence.

Brady brought his hand towards her neck, hesitating. 'We're not at work.' He let the words hang. 'May I? I just want to help...'

'Oh *really*.' Emma met his gaze and folded her arms, wondering what he intended, but determined to meet his bluff. 'Well then, by all means. If you only want to help.'

'Of course, that's all. Such sarcasm. Don't get all hot and bothered.' Brady grinned and carefully removed her name badge, drawing out the ordinary gesture into an intimate moment. He didn't touch her, but her breath left her body.

'I'm not h, h ... hot and ... What did you do that for?'

He leaned closer and whispered, 'Your name badge was upside down.' Handing it to her with a smile he walked away.

Emma fumed. The gall of the man. The absolute unmitigated hide of him. She should have given him a piece of her mind. And she would have. If she hadn't wanted so badly for him to kiss her.

Halfway

Ebony flashed through the room like a summer storm, dragging her ever-present bright pink backpack behind her. Brady sighed. She seemed to be avoiding his company, again.

'It's late.'

'I can tell time, Dad.'

'I hope you haven't been trying to get into clubs with Jenna and Bridget.'

'Clubs! Duh,' said Ebony looking at her frayed shorts and running shoes. 'I'm not demented, Dad.'

Swiftly retreating to her room, she put a Foo Fighters CD in the player and soon the music pounded through the closed door.

Steve looked up from his laptop. 'You worry too much.'

'What are you doing here still? Wasn't last night enough?'

Steve crossed his legs at the ankles and stuffed a pillow behind his head. 'But, but...my internet.' He smirked.

'These techno things don't get fixed overnight, old son.'

Brady groaned. 'I guess I asked for that.'

'How was your "not-a-date"?'

'We can't seem to help rubbing each other the wrong way; it's infuriating.'

'You mean she doesn't fall all over herself to impress you? Not a shrinking violet, our Emma.'

'No, that's for sure. She doesn't seem to care what anyone thinks, not just me.'

'That must be different for you.'

'What do you mean? I've met strong-minded people before. I get along fine with confident women.'

'Yeah, but I've never seen you attracted to one, mate.'

'Who says I'm attracted to her? I can't think about getting involved with anyone. Ebony comes first. I can't…'

'Give it a rest, Brady. You're an overprotective worrywart. And I do mean that in the nicest possible way.'

Brady met Steve's gaze. 'I know. You're right, Steve. Ebony doesn't need a babysitter.'

'No, she doesn't. Not just for an evening with Jim next door. Might be good to let her know that.'

'I was going to apologise, but she's snitchy with me. Things have changed. She's becoming rebellious. I should've seen this coming.'

'She is a teenager. Having little to say to one's parent and listening to loud music hardly qualifies as rebellion,' said Steve.

'Well, it looks like it's just around the corner. She talks to me as if I'm a retarded parrot,' muttered Brady.

'Well, you are a bit repetitive.'

'It's my job as a parent to be repetitive.'

'Yeah, sure. Look how that worked out for you. I remember a time when you were forbidden to take the train to Sydney. Now that's quite a story.'

'What's quite a story?' asked Ebony, poking her head around the corner.

Brady jumped. 'Fair go, Eb, don't sneak up on an old man. I didn't know you were there.'

'That's because I'm wearing *sneakers*, Dad, and not the kind of high heels we girls wear to clubs—when we're actually being rebellious. Anyway, what's this story, Uncle Steve? I could do with a dose of "my father was once human".'

'Don't you dare!' said Brady.

Steve smirked and settled comfortably into the sofa. 'It began like this...'

Brady grabbed Steve's baseball cap.

'That childish gesture won't get you anywhere, Brady. As I was saying...'

Ebony grinned and threw herself sideways into the sofa beside Brady. 'I'm all ears, Uncle Steve. Spill.'

Brady was so pleased to have his daughter next to him, and smiling, that he gave no further protest.

'Your father comes from a long line of men who were very silly as boys, but who grew up to become pillars of the community.'

Brady smiled. He could remember his grandmother telling him stories about his own father's childhood escapades. As a child Brady had been hard pressed to connect the stories of his father's wayward youth with the austere man who worked three jobs and tolerated no tom foolery from his own son. Brady had chafed at so many of the old fashioned phrases of his parents, but now he was a father the same words slipped unheeded from his mouth.

'It was your father's fifteenth birthday and he wanted to go to Sydney with his two best mates, Fang and Ratsy, with the marvellous plan of returning by train at 1:00 am.'

Emily giggled. 'Fang and Ratsy, well that bodes well. Heck, Dad. Fifteen, hey Dad?'

Brady flushed. The memory of that day flooded back.

His father had been furious. 'You're not travelling two hours on the train to Port Adelaide at your age. And especially not with those two mug lairs. Constable Todd caught them drinking outside the shopping mall. They're a bad influence,' Jim Harcourt stood, arms folded.

'Todd's a stupid old tosser. Why can't anyone in this place mind their own business? It's like living in a gold fish bowl. We've had this planned for weeks. Everyone will think I'm a baby,' moaned Brady.

His father calmly leaned on the door jamb. 'If they could hear you now they would think you are. Why don't you throw yourself on the floor? Make a proper show of yourself.'

'You never let me do what I want! You don't want me to have friends. You're ruining my life!' Brady voice rose and cracked in the tell-tale manner of the adolescent male, somewhat ruining the effect.

'Maybe next year, darling,' his mother Betty said softly as she twisted a tea towel.

'Maybe *not* next year, *darling,*' his father said, giving his wife a frosty stare. 'You're too soft on the boy, Betty. He'll get privileges when he acts responsibly, and not before. And when he's of an age to handle himself.'

Brady had huffed off out the door.

'He's just a boy. He'll grow out of it,' defended his mother.

The discussion of what was best for Brady was a pattern that played out over the course of their lives on wintry nights and lazy summer days alike. As an only child Brady rankled at the habit, wishing he had siblings to share the torment. He wouldn't have been the focus of his parents' lives; the guardian of their dreams. And more importantly, the cause of the disagreements that ebbed and flowed in the house like a restless familiar tide.

'What would they talk about if they hadn't had me?'

Brady had said to Steve. He'd gone to Steve's beach shack and was sitting on the veranda. 'It's like one of those chess games you play.'

'Well, I guess that makes you the pawn.' Steve's laugh was a low rumble. 'Anyway, last I heard you didn't want to go with them.'

'Well, that was before,' Brady stopped, embarrassed.

'Oh, the plot thickens. Before what, pray tell? It wouldn't have anything to do with Georgina Morgan, would it?'

The boy's tense silence was all the answer Steve needed.

'You don't actually think old man Morgan would let his precious daughter go on a train in the middle of the night with a bunch of hormonal teenage boys do you?'

Brady opened his mouth, then closed it again.

'You did!' Steve exclaimed. 'Let me tell you something about fathers and daughters, Sunshine. Fathers are complete saps when it comes to their daughters. But while they would give them their hearts desire inside the house—when it comes to going out that door, it's a whole other story.'

Brady was tempted to tell Steve that he was an old fogey like his father but he'd sounded like a pre-schooler once today. And it was dawning on him that Georgina's boast that her father would let her go might be ill conceived.

'You're as bad as them,' Brady said half-heartedly, rapidly losing steam.

'If you're spoiling for an argument you've come to the wrong place.' Steve grinned.

Brady sighed heavily. 'Stupid really, isn't it,' he conceded. 'I usually avoid arguments at home, but I'm always happy to start one here with you. For all the good it does me—you never argue back.'

'It's called the path of least resistance,' Steve responded indulgently.

'You'd be an expert on that,' muttered Brady.

They both laughed loudly, almost drowning out the crash of the surf that was metres from the weather-beaten veranda. Steve's own path of least resistance was more a lifestyle than a strategy. It had led him to a rambling rundown surf hut and surfboard-making business.

'Seriously though, Uncle Steve,' continued Brady earnestly. 'They only ever argue over the small stuff, trivial nonsense. Stuff about how I will turn out and who is doing the right thing by me. Hardly life changing. Their idea of fiscal management is—"If you don't have the money you don't need it". Brady mimicked his father's voice perfectly. 'They probably think "the old ordinaries" is a euphemism for second-hand underwear!'

'So you see, Ebony,' said Steve as he finished the story with relish, 'your stodgy old father wasn't always...'

'...stodgy,' laughed Ebony. 'Oh, thank you, Uncle Steve. 'There's hope for Dad yet.'

'Yes Steve, thanks very much,' said Brady, laughing. He threw Steve's cap out the front door. 'Now why don't you chase that!'

'Very mature, Dad,' said Ebony.

'See,' said Brady, 'No respect for her old man.'

'Oh, I see all right,' said Steve, snatching Brady's beer and swigging the last of it.

'With you two as role models there's no hope for me!' said Ebony.

Haunted

Emma stared out of the window of her office, grateful the day was over. She turned the radio volume up. Violent storms had ravaged the coast and she was worried about her staff on the roads.

The wind was increasing. Shards of lightning lit up the dim interior of the polyclinic, as thunder cracked.

A scream pierced the storm. Emma ran to the waiting area.

'Mummy's had an accident.' A little girl in a bright red raincoat had pushed open the side door from the carpark and was wailing.

'It's alright, sweetie. Where's mummy?' Emma bent down to the child.

'Out there.' The girl pointed. 'The baby's coming. She got pains real bad and crashed *bang*.' The girl slapped her hands together. 'Like that.'

Emma ran outside. A woman was sitting in a small white car. She'd backed into a car—Emma's Honda Civic. The woman's car door was open and she was crouched over the steering wheel.

'Are you all right?' Emma squatted by the car.

'Yes, I think so. Arrrgh. Contractions.' She gripped the steering wheel. 'Oh dear. I've hit someone.'

'Don't worry about that, let's get you some help.'

The afterhours GP wouldn't be on duty for another hour and most of the staff had left. Emma got her phone out and punched in Brady's number. He was still upstairs.

The woman grabbed Emma's hand. Brady flew out the side door and took in the scene. He picked up the girl and soothed her.

'We'll look after your mummy, honey. We've got to get her to a hospital, okay? But we'll phone your daddy and everything will be alright.'

The ambulance arrived in minutes, with the woman's husband roaring into the carpark while the paramedics assessed the woman.

'She's okay,' one of them said, 'but this baby's in a hurry. It's off to Maternity Ward for you sweetheart. Hold on.'

'Arrrgh!'

'Isn't that your car?' Brady wiped rain from his face. 'Come inside, Emma. You're shivering.'

'We're soaked.'

Inside, Emma found some hand towels. 'These won't be much use, but here.'

'Thanks, you looked in pain out there. Upset about your car?'

'I thought that poor woman was going to break my hand. I forgot how strong a woman in labour is.'

'Ah yes, I remember that!' Brady wiped at his face with the paper towels. 'Aren't there any proper towels in this place?'

'No, but I have some cotton blankets. I'll get those.'

'You'd better phone about your car. I'll give you a lift home.'

'I can get a taxi. It's late. Ebony will worry about you.'

'She won't even miss me. She's staying with Jenna tonight—a homework marathon.' He laughed. 'A con if ever I heard one.'

'She is a bit of a bookworm.'

'As long as she isn't studying that handsome son of Helena's.' Brady frowned.

'He's gone back to the city.'

'Ah, thank the universe for that. It's too soon to oil my shotgun. No one prepares you for that side of fatherhood.'

Emma reached for her mobile. Brady's hand covered hers. 'You'll wait ages for a taxi in this weather. You're soaking. Let me take you home.'

'Okay.'

After a few attempts at conversation over the pelting rain in the car, Brady and Emma gave up. Brady flicked the radio on, straining to hear the weather reports, although it also struggled to compete with the storm. Even with the wipers on full, it was hard to see ahead. Brady slowed. He stared ahead, intent on the road. Emma leaned forward. She didn't want to miss the turn-off to her home. It was a long dirt road, and the streetlights were sparse.

'It's just around the next bend,' she said. 'There are two driveways close together, mine's the one on the right. You can drop me at the entrance. It's not far, I'm already drenched.'

'Thick as pea soup out there,' Brady said, as the car purred into her driveway. 'I'll see you to the door.'

Emma shot him a quick look. Brady's face gave nothing away as he reached across her to open her car door. She was instantly aware of his warmth and the scent of him. She shivered. 'You're cold.' He pulled the cotton blanket around her.

She fumbled with the keys and Brady took them from her and patiently jiggled the key in the lock and opened the door.

'Are you going to invite me in? For a ... cup of cyanide?' He smiled, his eyes lazily watching her.

Emma laughed. 'You're sure you wouldn't prefer strychnine? I have a lovely caramel one.' She threw the door open.

Brady whistled. 'Wow! This is quite a place. How did you get a pad like this on a nurse's wage? Rob a bank?'

'Several.' Emma opened a cupboard. 'I might take a while to find things. I haven't been here long.'

'How long?'

'Only a month.' Emma opened another overhead cupboard.

'Jeez! That long. You must be really busy, or...oh dear, are you all right?'

Tears streamed down Emma's face.

Brady moved quickly to her and tilted her face up. 'What's wrong Emma? Did I say something? I'm sorry, I can be such a dufus at times.'

'It's just, it's just...Oh, I'm sorry.' She gave in to a torrent of tears that had been threatening for months.

Gently cradled in his arms, Brady let her cry it out.

Eventually the sobbing stopped. Emma wiped the back of her hand over her eyes and smiled shyly at him. 'I didn't know I was going to bawl over you.'

'Some tears are really sneaky like that.'

'There's all kinds, isn't there.'

'You bet. Been there, done that. So, do you want to talk about it?'

'I was just standing here thinking I couldn't even make you a proper cup of coffee because I've never used the fancy coffee machine. I haven't really used the place at all. It feels all wrong. I love the unit, I mean, but...I only have it because my fiancé died. I can't let myself feel at home.'

'That makes sense.'

145

'Does it? I feel like it's the stupidest thing, not to be able to live in the home I've chosen. Ben would want me to enjoy it, but I can't. Oh dear, I'm sorry. Your shirt is all wet. We're all wet.'

'Well, my shirt had nearly dried until you cried all over it.' He grinned.

She smiled, grateful for his understanding. 'I'll get some robes. Thank goodness it was warm summer rain, but I'm a bit chilly now.'

She left the room and came back with two fluffy robes, one silver grey and the other bright pink. She gave him a cheeky look. 'Which one would you prefer?'

'Oh, that's easy,' he said, 'I'll take pink any chance I get.' Retrieving the robe, he threw off his shirt and slipped into it. 'Oh my God, what is this thing made of? It's the most comfortable thing I've ever worn—is it impregnated with drugs? I must warn you I take a very strong stand on illegal substances.'

'Gorgeous isn't it.'

'It's beyond gorgeous. I may steal it.'

'Not gay are you?'

Brady sighed. With his eyes pinned on her, he came slowly towards her. All playfulness was gone and his gaze seared her. Emma couldn't breathe. He was inches away. Neither spoke. He pressed his lips to hers. There was no tentativeness in his caress. He grasped her shoulders. With lazy sensuality he explored her sweetness, then with ragged breath, draw back. Emma shivered and leaned into him.

'I'm not apologising for that,' he said, when his breathing returned to normal. He tilted her chin until she looked straight into his eyes. 'I'm a free man, no matter what you thought you saw at the beach concert, and I've been longing to do that since I first saw you.'

'Oh.' Emma touched his face.

'I'm a patient man, one with self-control. I can wait. I think you need me here tonight. To lay the ghosts of the past to rest.' One hand caressed her neck, then he stepped back.

'I ... well, you probably shouldn't drive home in this storm.' Emma lowered her eyes.

'Do you want me to stay, Emma?'

'Yes, please Brady. But...' Her voice was a whisper.

'I understand. I'll be a perfect gentleman.'

She breathed out slowly, and smiled softly.

'Are you hungry? I'm famished.' Brady prowled around the kitchen and opened the fridge. 'Ooh, bacon and eggs.'

'Oh, that would be wonderful,' she said. 'I forgot about food.'

'Really?' Brady assessed her coolly.

She looked down, embarrassed that he could read her. 'I don't know where the pans and things are. Sorry.'

'Don't worry. You whizz into the shower, while I cook

up a storm. Then you can serve up while I jump in for a quick warm up. Please tell me you know where the towels are? Those cotton holey things are soaked through. They weigh a ton wet.'

Emma disappeared into the downstairs bathroom.

Brady got busy in the kitchen. It took him a while to find everything. Emma must have just thrown things anywhere in the cupboards. Not that she had much in the way of cooking gear. He liked that, he was a minimalist himself. He noticed everything she had was good quality.

They didn't speak through the meal; then when they were sated, they leaned back in the kitchen chairs. Brady decided to keep wearing the pink gown, it was infused with her perfume, a subtle, earthy smell—not too sweet or heavy.

'That was great, thanks Brady,' said Emma, yawning.

'You're welcome. Now show me this haunted bedroom you can't sleep in.'

She led the way up the timber staircase.

'Wow! I didn't think the upstairs could live up to the rest, but this is great. I bet the view is wonderful. This backs on to the national park doesn't it?'

'Yes, the bush is quite spectacular. The neighbours have a birdbath and feed the native birds. It's quite something to wake up to birdsong every morning.'

'Well, you've made the bed at least. I thought you nurses never made your own beds?' He threw himself on the bed and bounced around. 'Not bad suspension. I can work with this.' It was killing him to be casual, but he didn't want to spook her.

'Um, Brady...Is that, er, robe tied properly?'

'Oh, for Lar's, girl. You'll no be getting a view of the weddin' vegetables tonight even if ye beg me. I've got me flannels on, to be sure. Joseph and Mary, what kind of a fella do ye take me fer? You get under the sheets and I'll stay on top. I'll be as silent as the grave itself, indeed I will.'

Emma giggled uncontrollably. 'You make a terrible Scotsman.'

Brady pulled the robe between his legs in mock horror, crawled further to the edge of the bed, and turned to face the windows. A soft blanket was draped over him. Then he felt her slide onto the bed, tense, then relax, with an infectious giggle bursting out every few minutes.

'Wedding vegetables! Honestly! I've never heard that.' Another giggle followed.

'How's a man to get any sleep with all that cackling?'

'Sorry. And you don't need to lie so close to the edge. I don't want you falling out in the night.'

'Oh, I don't know, a man can't be too careful. I'm afraid of being ravaged in the night. Any woman that gives a man a pink robe is dangerous. Anyway, it's morning if you care to look. Which is long past time for sleeping.'

Nonetheless Brady wriggled back from the edge and

settled into a comfortable position. He breathed deeply, feigning sleep.

Emma heard his deep breathing and sighed. Moments later she was fast asleep.

Brady heard her gentle snore, and willed himself to sleep, to no avail. She'd taken him by surprise. He was becoming attracted to her at a far deeper and more dangerous level than just admiring her looks and personality. He liked her—all of her.

She was resilient, independent, warm and funny. He tried breathing deeply again. Her scent on the robe smelt wonderful. Maybe it wasn't such a good idea to wear hers. That combined with her nearness and his growing need for her meant he'd probably get no sleep at all.

And that kiss, that kiss.

A door

'Ebony, put that book away, you must be nearly asleep. You haven't turned a page in ages. Maybe it's time to think of bed?'

'Father, with some books you keep reading the same sentence over and over because it won't stick in your head, but other times you just want to taste it again and again.' Ebony placed the open book face down in her lap. 'Haven't you ever felt that way about a book?'

'You know, I can't remember.'

'Come on Dad, there must have been at least one book.'

'Do computer magazines count,' asked Brady.

Ebony groaned and put her hands over her face. 'Honestly, Dad, just when I think there's hope for you, you come out with something like that!'

Brady quelled his response. His daughter was sharing with him. even though he had no idea what the point of the conversation was, it was a connection. He put his newspaper down, took his reading glasses off and regarded his daughter.

'Am I that bad, Eb? An illiterate uptight Neanderthal?'

Ebony smiled. 'I didn't say that.'

'But you did say that you sometimes think there's hope for me...'

'Oh. You noticed?'

'Of course, kiddo.'

Ebony smiled. Brady's heart constricted, her smile was reminiscent of the past—those days when her adoration of him was something he took for granted.

'I love that smile. Where has it been?'

She groaned, 'That's so lame, Dad.'

'I've lost my touch, haven't I? Go on then, read to me. Teach an old dog new tricks.'

Ebony settled into the sofa with her head resting on her hand. The fire glowed amber. The wood crackled, sending sparks into the air. Her voice was soft and mellow, her expression alive with enjoyment as she began.

> 'It is so tiresome to escape one's governess, don't you find, Cousin Eloisa?' said Jane, as both girls sat swinging their legs from the low thick branch of a spreading oak. 'Thank goodness it is summer—in winter the trees are next to useless for hiding places.'

'Now, Dad don't roll your eyes! You asked for this.'

'I'm not...You can't tell—you weren't even looking at me.'

Ebony gave her father a look of reproach and Brady obediently gestured that he was zipping his lips.

'I guess it could be a nuisance escaping one's governess, Cousin Jane, but as I have so recently acquired one—courtesy of your generous family, I have not yet found it more than an entertaining pastime. And "escaping", as you call it, has helped us discover the most magical places, like this marvellous old oak tree,' said Eloisa. 'You know, cousin, it seems quite at odds with polite convention to call one's governess by her surname, especially as Gantry is such a horrible name. I wonder, do all the gentry follow that custom? It is all very confusing for a newcomer, but I must say that on first impression, a governess seems more concerned for the well-being of her charges than one's own mother would. Of course, as an orphan, I know nothing of that.'

'Oh, I am so sorry, Cousin Eloisa. I did not intend to bring up your sadness or refresh your grief, how thoughtless of me. Please forgive me.'

'Now, **that** is tiresome, dear Cousin Jane. Pity is a grievous burden. You cannot imagine how dreadful it is for everyone to constantly cast you in the light of an eternal victim of tragic circumstances. Is that how I am to be introduced for the rest of my life? Is that all people will ever whisper about? Will I ever be simply me, Eloisa Lancaster? I wonder if I shall ever shake it

153

off. Perhaps I could move to France...'

Jane frowned. 'You know, Cousin Eloisa, you are really rather odd.'

'Well, that is a far better description to live with. You know, Cousin Jane, I think you are on to something. If I develop an interesting persona, people will have something else to focus on. I would rather be known for any number of eccentricities than as a poor soul blighted by life, and fit for nothing but pity in society.'

Jane was perplexed. Her cousin had only been living with them for several months and had given no sign of this new alarming side of her character. After an initial feeling of finally having the sister-in-spirit she had always longed for, and deciding that she and Eloisa were as near to kindred spirits as two people could be, she was shocked to realise that she did not understand her cousin at all. Never short of a word, she now found herself speechless and was rather pleased when their portly governess appeared over the hill, with her long aprons and skirts held high, sweating profusely. Heaving herself in front of the two girls, Gantry pressed one hand on her ample bosom and panted. Her face was red with exertion as she fanned her face with a muslin handkerchief.

Jane leapt out of the tree, instantly contrite.

'You frightful girls! Why do you play these games?

Gallivanting all over the estate. You shall return to the house this instant and sit quietly reading, while I retire to my room to recover.'

Jane opened her mouth to apologise, but Eloisa cut in, 'If it is all the same to you, dear Gantry, I will repose awhile in the midst of the splendour of this magnificent monument to nature. After all, only minutes before we left to "occupy ourselves until nuncheon" as you instructed, you told us that we would ruin our eyes if we read another paragraph. I am new to having a governess and do not wish to give you any cause for concern. I am sure you will be pleased that now we have gallivanted all over the estate you can forego our afternoon ambulation. I shall wish you sweet rest, dear Gantry. I will certainly be back in the...er...nursery, when you awaken and arise.'

With that, Eloisa focused on an interesting spot on the horizon and began to hum.

Jane was incredulous and Gantry stood open-mouthed with shock.

'Well, I never!' huffed Gantry. 'I am sure I do not know what to say to your High and Mightiness Miss Eloisa. We shall see about this.' Firmly grasping Jane's hand she turned to leave.

Jane threw Eloisa a disconcerted look.

Eloisa winked.

Ebony stopped reading, but her eyes remained on the page. The room was silent except for the sounds of the rolling surf in the background.

Brady cleared his throat. 'I see what you mean,' he said. 'It does have a certain charm.'

Ebony blinked. He was obviously moved by something in the story. Just when she thought she had him figured out, he changed. Maybe he was thawing out. It might have something to do with Emma. She still hoped he'd be attracted to the nurse.

She'd been dropping enough hints and he had spent some time with Emma. Maybe she'd given him some Dadzilla-altering pills. What else would account for dear old Dad tearing up over a bit of chick lit? *Ancient* chick lit at that.

'Well, I'm off to bed,' she said.

'Turn the light off on your way out, will you Eb?'

Ebony shrugged. 'You want me to leave you in the dark? Whatever.' Her father was back to being weird again.

Brady sat in the dark, alone with his thoughts. *Pity is a grievous burden.* Something inside broke free, lifting him towards possibility, towards understanding. His daughter had shared something with him, something larger than the words she'd read. He recognised the beauty of the moment, its frailty and perfection. As he left the room, he turned to the book. 'Goodnight, Cousin Eloisa.'

With you

Brady stared at his watch. Emma would be there soon. Autumn was late arriving, but the summer crowds at the kiosk had thinned. Shading his eyes, he looked out to the ocean. The roar of the surf was punctuated with the wet slap of waves on sand. Clean white froth met pale gamboge as the sea bubbled up through the sand, tickling it into life as the pull of the salt water began its eternal cycle out to the ocean.

'Sorry, I'm late.'

Brady rose and drew Emma close for a searching kiss.

'Would you do something for me?' she asked.

'Anything. Right arm or left?'

Emma smiled. 'I'd like a double choc berry fudge sundae, please. I'll just walk down to the bench and wait there for you okay?'

'That bench? The infamous bench—where I first saw you and made such a lasting impression?'

'That's the one,' Emma laughed.

'So what can I do you for, mate?' asked the kiosk attendant. He was a large jovial guy with a broad grin.

Brady gave the order precisely.

'Sort that knows your mind then?'

Brady smiled at the staccato conversation. 'Not always, mate, but it's ice cream right?'

'Yeah, how hard can it be? You'd be surprised. Some take ages. You look like a guy who knows what he wants.'

'Clear as mud, really.'

The man shrugged. 'That's life, eh. What's the song you've been humming, mate? S'familiar. Wife used to sing it.'

'Sorry, bit embarrassing. Um, 'I only want to be with you', yeah, that's it—must have heard it on the radio,' said Brady who hadn't listened to the radio in years.

'Right. Sure. Nothin' to do with the cute blonde, of course.'

'Well...'

'Ya don't have to tell me, mate.' The man winked, and turned to serve another customer.

Walking down to Emma, Brady was mesmerised by her stillness, the midday sun made her hair glow. Her back was to him, and even without seeing her face, his heart quickened.

'Oh, hi. Yum, that looks good.' Emma had turned and the smile that lit her face spread through Brady like warm honey.

'You're beautiful,' he said. 'Did you know that?'

'Ah...Why thank you, Brady Harcourt. What a wonderful time to be told—over a chocolate sundae. A man wouldn't lie in the middle of the day with a chocolate sundae.'

'With nuts, cream and fudge sauce, and a waffle triangle thingy.' They began to walk along the beach.

'And I thought you only had a good memory for figures.'

'There are all kinds of figures,' he said. 'And yours is *so fine.*'

'Brady Harcourt, you're flirting with me.'

'Glad you noticed. You can give me a score if you like. I'm out of practice.'

Emma tilted her head. Dipping the waffle triangle into the rich fudge, she licked the gooey sauce. Brady's eyes darkened. Emma swallowed hard. The air between them changed.

'Are you practising on me?' Emma stopped dead still.

Brady moved slowly towards her. 'You have...fudge sauce, here...' He brushed a finger across her bottom lip to wipe away the sauce then licked his finger '...and here'. Emma drew in a ragged breath. Placing one arm around her he drew her into the shadows of the old boat shed. Then, leaning on the dry cracked wall, he pulled her against him. He inched her closer, gently, tenderly, his eyes never leaving hers. Allowing only a breath between their mouths he paused, willing her to him.

Two chocolate sundaes hit the sand as Brady closed the gap and kissed her thoroughly. He knew the exact moment of her surrender. It felt like the first time he'd taken the lead in the dance of love, and the feeling was intoxicating.

His exploration of her mouth delved deeper, stronger. Keeping his passion in check, he kissed her neck, nuzzling her shell pink earlobes. She sighed, melting into him. He was master. There was no hesitation in his caresses, no ambiguity, and as if to reassure her, he whispered her name over and over.

'Brady...'

'I'm falling for you Emma. It's too late for you to tell me that it's too soon. It's...'

'You know something Brady—you're better at the kissing bit, than the talking.'

They walked back to the kiosk.

'Dad, I'm glad we found you,' said Ebony.

'Were you looking for me?' asked Brady.

'Well, no, but now we've bumped into you both.' Ebony stared at her father holding Emma's hand.

Jenna rolled effortlessly in backwards circles on her roller blades around the group.

'Hi Jenna,' said Emma, 'You're pretty good on those roller blades. You could teach me a thing or two.'

'Anyway,' said Ebony, 'Dad, the radio has just announced they're giving away free tickets to "Rough Steel". They're going to be in Eiredale next month and the radio guy is giving out tickets at...'

'Who?'

'Just listen, Dad. If we hurry we'll get there in time.'

'Where? Eiredale.'

'No, Dad! You're not paying attention. Johnno from FM 186 is at the Esplanade Hotel at Brighton.'

'And what if I don't want you to go to the concert, or whatever it is. Have you thought of that?'

'Always, Dad. Always.' Ebony rolled her eyes and was rewarded with an elbow in the ribs by Jenna whose parental manipulation skills were far superior, and she saw their chances taking a nosedive.

'You can get the tickets, Mr Harcourt,' she said, 'They're freebies. And if you don't want us to have them, you can give them away. Talk to Jack if you like.'

Brady moaned and reached for the car keys.

'You coming, Emma? Please? Don't leave an old fart with these hyperactive delinquents.' Brady posed his hands in a prayer.

'Yes, Emma, please come!' said Ebony. There was no time to waste. 'The radio jocks usually only stay in one place for half an hour.'

Brady and Emma headed for the car, with Brady claiming her hand again.

Ebony grabbed Jenna's arm. 'What's with the *Mister* Harcourt bit, Jenna? That was a bit over the top,' she said.

'It worked, didn't it? Hurry up and get your blades off. You are such a newbie. Acting lessons wouldn't go astray in your case.'

'Bite me.'

Brady smiled. He'd never seen the girls get in the car so fast. He looked across at Emma as the car purred into motion. For a short time contentment had arrived in his world, and he wasn't going to question it. He wanted to keep holding Emma's hand as he would have done in his teenage years, but it didn't seem the thing to do. He didn't know how Ebony felt about his feelings for Emma.

He knew Ebony liked Emma, but a relationship with her father? She hadn't reacted well to Julia Prescott's presence on Australia Day. He hoped that was because Julia had behaved like a possessive already-girlfriend, and not because Ebony would resent any new woman.

Emma stretched out languidly in the passenger seat, content to let the girls' animated conversation in the back fill the car. Brady liked that about her. She didn't try to compete or seek attention. She was warming to him, but the depth of her feelings was still a mystery. She was in no hurry, and that made Brady impatient for the first time in his life. Impatient to hold her, have her, make her his own.

He tried to put a pause to his errant thoughts, his body was growing warm with desire. It wasn't helped by the nearness of the soft curves of her tanned legs against white shorts and tattered sneakers. Scarlett would have dressed to impress, but it seemed the last thing on Emma's mind.

Revelation

Pandemonium reigned at the Esplanade car park. The girls were out of the car even faster than they had climbed in only minutes before. For a moment Brady panicked as he saw the two girls disappear into the crowd.

'Don't worry,' said Emma, 'these things never last long.'

'But I don't see any security.'

'Brady Harcourt, you're more of a worrywart than I thought, I must sign you up for our mother's group at the clinic.'

'Oh great,' he moaned. 'Hey! Are there any hot babes in this mother's thing?'

Emma laughed. 'They're all absolute foxes.'

'I'm crushed,' said Brady. 'You're not even a little bit jealous?' He held up his thumb and forefinger a few millimetres apart.

Emma merely smiled. 'Are you going to get out and check up on the girls?'

'I'd look a right prat, wouldn't I?'

'Hallelujah, the boy learns.'

'We could make out.'

'I only ever intend to be kissed thoroughly, Brady Harcourt. No snatched moments.'

'I get it.'

'Good, then I might just tip the sand out of my sneakers.'

Brady forgot about the rest of the world and the noise outside as Emma leant out of the car, removing first one shoe, then the other as she emptied the sand onto the tarred surface and brushed her feet with slow, elegant hands. He imagined those hands on him. His hand clenched the wheel. Who knew such a simple gesture could be so sensuous? A soft curtain of hair covered Emma's face and he longed to deliver those thorough kisses she'd mentioned. *Those are mine,* he thought. *All of them.*

The girls arrived back at the car pink-faced and chattering with excitement. Brady smiled. It was a long time since he had seen Ebony so animated. Life was slowly turning. As the girls shared the spoils of their conquest in the back seat Brady stole a quick tender kiss with Emma, then secured his seat belt.

'Look, two CD's by Rough Steel,' said Jenna, waving them in triumph as Ebony tried to snatch them.

'One's mine,' said Ebony.

'I'll toss you for the choice,' said Jenna.

Ebony considered the idea with a rueful twist of the mouth, 'Okay.'

'Why didn't you girls want to stay and have lunch at the hotel?' asked Brady.

'Duh!' said Ebony, shaking a huge plastic bag displaying the radio logo above her head. She had a green jelly snake drooping from either side of her mouth and a goofy grin.

Jenna crunched loudly on crisps.

'Okay, I surrender—come on share the loot,' said Brady, reaching his hand as far back into the car as he could from the driver's seat with the constraints of the seatbelt.

He was rewarded with a gooey mess of melted jellies and a cacophony of giggling.

'Arrggh, yuk!' he said.

'You asked for that,' said Emma, smiling. She pulled a wet disposable cloth out of her handbag and took the gelatinous lump, wiping his hand at the same time.

'How do women do that?' said Brady. 'You must carry half a house in your handbags. You would have made a good boy scout.'

'You cheeky...' Emma tucked the wet cloth into the neck of his T shirt and sat back, arms folded.

'You'll keep,' said Brady, his eyes full of sly promise. He left the cloth there and opened the sun roof. The car was instantly filled with cool autumn air. The girls squealed in delight as their hair was lifted gently in the breeze.

Brady covered his ears in mock horror and muttered, 'females'.

The road through the Onkaparinga Hills was beautiful. As the road wound through bushland and rural paddocks, the glint of the ocean sparkled. The early afternoon sun seemed to follow them. The road curved upward and the shrubs were replaced with tall gums, heralding the homeward stretch.

Brady leaned back in satisfaction, grateful to the universe for one perfect day.

The traffic was heavier now.

The van in front showed red brake lights. Instantly alert, Brady pressed slowly on the brakes and then hit them with all his force as the car in front stopped dead.

'Dad!' shrieked Ebony, as fruit gels, wrapped sweets and crisps flew through the car.

Brady leaned over the steering wheel, but could see nothing beyond the large van. Then the van accelerated past a car parked on the gravel shoulder and stopped just beyond it.

'Oh my God,' said Emma, unconsciously grasping Brady's thigh. 'There's been an accident.'

A small blue car with a mangled rear end was skewed

at a strange angle on the verge. A surfboard lay on the ground beyond, broken, free from its tangled ropes.

Two workmen leapt out of the van that had been ahead of them and one immediately took up a position to warn and direct traffic. Brady parked carefully in front of the van. Emma was out of the car in an instant.

The first sound that Brady heard was a guttural moaning that echoed through the trees. He was too disorientated by his own shocked senses to ascertain its origin, but instinctively followed Emma.

'I'm a nurse,' she said to the first man from the van, who nodded towards the passenger side of the car, as he threw open the driver's door. The driver's seat was empty. A young man was slumped in the passenger seat, unconscious, his breathing a laboured whistle. His forehead and face were stained with blood. Emma ran to the passenger side and began to pull on the door handle. It was stuck tight. The impact had skewed the chassis.

Brady looked down at his feet and fought nausea as he saw the driver lying beside the car. The angle of his neck and the position of his limbs left little doubt. Struggling to clear his head, he worked wordlessly with the man from the van to carry the man's lifeless body onto the grassy area beside the car.

Another car stopped. Voices rose and fell. Emma asked for a blanket. A woman ran to her car boot and retrieved one. Someone phoned for help, someone placed a tarpaulin over the dead man, and still the loud groaning continued.

'What's that?' Brady turned to the man from the van, who jerked a thumb in the direction of a small quarry. Brady nodded. 'I'll go.'

There was a small removal hire truck. And a man. Brady had never seen such agitation. The man was alternately leaning forward, tearing at his hair and hitting bloodied fists against the truck. A small brunette was trying fruitlessly to restrain and comfort him. Brady approached the man and endeavoured to hold him in the manner he had learned with the clients at the youth centre, but the man reacted wildly, flaying his arms and groaning even louder.

'Leave him,' said the woman, 'he's out of it.' She returned to circling the man, focused on him, tears streaming down her face.

Feeling useless, Brady returned to the other car and the gathering crowd. He heard murmured phrases in different voices, and slowly the picture of events formed in his mind. The truck driver had fallen asleep at the wheel and hit the car. The driver of the blue car had been leaning into the boot and had taken the full impact of the crash. He had died instantly. Someone had partially covered him with a green tarpaulin.

Like a compass he sought Emma. She was wiping blood from the passenger's face and crooning softly to him. Another woman stood nearby. She was shaken. 'What can I do? I'm a nurse too, but I've never seen an accident, not...'

Jenna wandered up from the car.

'No, Jenna!' said Brady.

'I'm okay,' she said, stumbling over a protruding leg of the dead man and then joining Emma.

Other voices intruded.

'poor bastards...'

'anyone know them...?'

'any ID...?'

'mad with grief...'

'no hope for this one either...'

'someone's sons'

'there's the ambulance...'

'police too...

It was then Brady saw Ebony throwing up by a tree. He ran to her and held her tight, tears stinging his eyes. All thought was lost as he cleaned the face of his child, turned her from the scene to protect her.

Ebony cried tears then, real tears torn from deep within as she clutched her father with an iron grip. Brady pulled her closer, cradling her head and lightly stroking her hair back from her eyes as she buried her face into his neck.

The sun hid behind a lone wandering cloud. A chill shuddered through the air.

Emma and Jenna came down to them.

Jenna was chattering lightly to Emma about how she had hung out on set with the television company nurse. 'I thought I might become...' she stopped suddenly when she saw Ebony and Brady. Her mouth formed an 'o' and she looked to Emma. Emma guided her towards the car. When father and daughter arrived Emma and Jenna were ready to take the back seats.

Brady shot Emma a quick grateful glance.

The trip home was silent, each of them lost in their own thoughts. The sun's rays were slanting through the trees now and Brady wondered how long they had been gone. It seemed like a lifetime.

At home, Ebony went straight to her room, answering Brady's gently enquiry of 'Do you want to talk about it, Eb?' with 'I think I need to sleep.'

Brady's heart fell. He sat in the small front sitting room, choosing a sofa that gave him a view of Ebony's closed door. It was some connection, some comfort, even though her silent exit had pained him. He had hoped she would want to talk, but her message was clear. Adjusting his glasses he picked up a newspaper but couldn't concentrate. He wanted to talk to Emma, but his need to be near his daughter overruled. Emma would understand.

Ebony's tears were silent now as she clutched her pillow tightly to her chest. She felt a pang at the memory of her father's face as she had walked away from him minutes ago, but how could she talk to him about today, about anything when there was so much that weighed on her, so much ground between. Ground he didn't even seem to comprehend.

None of them had known the cause for her agony, she was sure of that—they would have assumed it was the horror of the victims that brought her reaction, but she hadn't even seen them. She hadn't been close enough. She'd been too frozen in the agony of the man who had been driving the truck. The man who'd killed two people. The man with questions that would later find harsh, brutal answers.

Ebony wondered if any penalty that would be given to him would ever compare to the grief and pain he suffered from the consequences of a few moments lapse in time. She cried for him, but not just for him, for the nameless man who had killed her mother. How she had hated him over the years—the faceless man who took her mother's life, changed a family forever, leaving a gap that couldn't be filled; and leaving questions, so many questions.

She wanted to drift off to sleep—to peace, but the face of the driver wouldn't shift. He had a name, a family. He was someone. Never again would she be able to shield herself behind a barrier of anger and bitterness about that other driver. Her stomach cramped. She was ashamed for what she had carried. Life had changed that afternoon.

The words she had thrown so often to Jenna 'the truth will set you free' seemed so trite now. She experienced scorn for her simplistic attitude.

She remembered her mother's answer to everything, 'You'll understand when you grow up, Ebony.'

Suddenly she realised that her mother had been more withdrawn and unaware than her father on his worst day. Her father. How close he had held her. Did he realise he'd been humming the words from 'Les Miserables' when Eponine died in Maruis' arms? 'I will keep you safe...'

By holding onto the memory of that moment she was finally able to drift into restless slumber.

A few feet away Brady was stretched out in the chair wondering why Ebony was humming. The tune stirred a memory, but it escaped as soon as he reached for it.

Awry

'I don't know why I can't help out in your office, Jack. I might even be able to get permission from school to do work experience with you. Then I could fill in for Helena. Come on, Dad.' Jenna sat across from her father.

Jack raked fingers through his hair.

'I don't think it's a good idea, Jenna. Everything in there is confidential. What would people think if I had a teenager as an office assistant? I have to go out of the office a lot. I couldn't leave you then. My business would go down the gurgler in a New York minute. I'll get a temp in if I have to. I know Helena's been doing too much. Full time in my office, and some of the field work.'

'That's where I could help,' said Jenna, with huge innocent eyes. 'Surely there's some small part I could do?'

'Persistent miss, aren't you.'

'Wonder where I get that from?'

Jenna gathered their plates together, stacking the rubbish neatly on top.

'You're a tidy little thing. Didn't get that from me.' Jack

smiled. 'You know, I wonder what you two girls are up to at times. This sudden interest in my work. I don't think you're looking at becoming a private investigator as a career choice. I always thought you'd follow in your mother's footsteps and take up acting.'

'Oh really, Jack? Why does everyone assume that? That's the last career I'd want. And let's face it— Madeleine's footsteps? The angst and insecurity. No thanks. I'm thinking of becoming a vet and opening my own practice. I'd need business skills for that.'

Jack stood, rolling his eyes. 'If that's another hint.'

'Me? Hint?'

Helena came into the room. 'You haven't been at your father to help in the office again, have you Jenna? He might have a blind spot when it comes to you, but you're up to something,' she said.

'I have to do work experience somewhere.'

Jack sighed. 'Well, if you want to be a vet you could probably help out at the veterinary clinic across town.'

'Yes, Jenna. You'd love that,' said Helena. 'Anyway, why don't you get into your homework? Your father and I have to go out tonight. There's a fundraiser for the youth centre.'

'I'm waiting for Ebony. We'll get stuck into our homework. She'll be here soon. She and her dad bought bikes. Can you believe it's Ebony's first bike, like ever! Incredible, isn't it?'

'Bye darling,' said Jack, putting his arm around Helena. Jenna blew them air kisses and shut the door.

'It's no good. I can't get around Dad,' said Jenna. 'I can't even get his keys. He would've made a good spy.'

'Well, it was worth a try. Silly really; you can't get access to your Dad's office, and I can't find the truth,' said Ebony.

'The truth about what? I mean if I'm going to help you, I should know.' Jenna leaned back on the bed.

'So much stuff. Stuff about Mum and the night she died. Things don't add up. There would be software and databases in your dad's office. Oh I don't know. Jack must have some special kind of access to records. Dad hasn't told me much. That was okay when I was twelve, I get it. But now? What's he trying to hide? Can't he tell how important it is? I mean, I'm his daughter.'

'Have you asked your dad? I mean really asked him to sit down and talk about it all?'

Ebony shrugged. 'It's not just that night.'

'What do you mean?'

'I worry, you know.' Ebony tugged at her hair. 'What would I say anyway? "Dad, what was Mum doing the night she died? Sneaking out to see some other guy?" I've heard the rumours. That she might have deliberately walked in front of that truck. Did she want to die? I can't ask him that sort of stuff.'

'Have you ever considered that your dad might not know? He just doesn't seem the sort of guy to hide things, I'm just sayin'.'

'It's possible. But "I don't know" is an answer. Silence is just rubbish. As good as a lie.'

'You have a point. Well, we'll just have to think of another way to get information. We should make a list of questions.' Jenna twirled her hair around a slim finger. 'If you're sure you want to do this.'

Ebony hesitated. She slowly pulled a faded silk jewellery pouch from her backpack.

'What's that?' asked Jenna.

Ebony untied the satin ribbon and took out a small ring box. Opening it she showed it to Jenna.

'Oh, wow! That's the biggest ruby I've ever seen. Where did you get it?'

'It was in a box of Mum's photographs. Dad and I had a row over the photos when we moved in, but I hung them up anyway. I don't know what his deal was, it was like he was ashamed of her.'

'The photos in your bedroom?'

'Yeah.'

'But they're beautiful. Why would he be upset about that?'

'Some rubbish about how he remembered her. I dunno.'

'I guess they are kinda sad. But they are in your room,

it's not as if he has to even look at them.'

'I know. There's other stuff too. I was going to show him, but he made such a fuss about the photos I kept the box in my room. And I found these.' Ebony held up a folder. It contained a sheet of parchment paper. It was a letter of notification of a scholarship to study at a prestigious art school in Sydney. The name Scarlett Harcourt was written in rich elegant script.

Jenna held it, and read it.

'Wow, this is really something. Your Mum must've been thrilled.'

'But don't you see? It doesn't make any sense. She always wanted to go back to study art. This was her big chance. They gave so few of these out, but she never even told us about it.'

'What's the big deal?'

'She got the letter a few weeks before she died.'

'Oh. That is weird.'

'She wouldn't have killed herself—not with this opportunity that she'd waited so long for, but why didn't she tell us? I have to know.'

'Maybe she didn't want to jinx it.'

Ebony sighed. 'I worry, you know.'

'What do you mean, worry about what?' asked Jenna.

'Well, not just about what happened, how she died and that. I worry that I might...you know, be like her one day.'

'You think bipolar is inherited?'

'I don't know. No one talks about it. It's scary, knowing what she went through, how hard it was for her to cope. I tried to watch that she took her medication, but she hid things, like, *really well.*'

'But not everyone with bipolar lives like that. Mum has some friends with it and they enjoy life like everyone else.'

'But I need facts. First about how she died, and about this ring. I want to know why Dad is so sensitive about talking about her, not the nitty gritty of their marriage, none of that stuff, just something to tell me who I am. He won't tell me, so I have to find out myself.'

'I didn't realise you were worrying about all this. I thought it was just about the accident.' Jenna shrugged. 'You said you wanted the newspapers around the time she died and that's why we were checking out libraries. The old duck at the council library was no help.' Jenna sat up. 'Hang on, what about the school library? They're supposed to have a newspaper records department. Didn't you want to find out what was in the papers after your mum died? Let's check there. Shouldn't be too hard to pretend to that airhead librarian we're doing school research.'

'Thanks, Jenna,' said Ebony, 'this means a lot.'

'Don't mention it. I can't think why I ever thought life in the antipodes would be boring.'

'Me neither.'

'Emma!' Jenna grabbed her friend's hand. 'I have the

most brilliant idea. I don't know why I didn't think of it before. We can go to the school library now.'

'What! You call that brilliant! Have you lost your mind! The school closed hours ago, and...'

'Oh, come on, Emma, it's the perfect time. We won't get another chance like this. You said you wanted answers.' Jenna swung her feet impatiently. 'Don't be tiresome.'

'I don't know. It's, well, there's just so much that could go wrong.'

'Okay,' said Jenna, 'here's the thing.' She lifted up both hands and held onto her left forefinger with her right hand in a gesture that was now familiar and alarming. Jenna was in hyper-logical, nothing-can-go-wrong mode.

Ebony sighed.

'One,' Jenna continued, 'we haven't found out anything about the accident other than your mother was hit by a truck late at night. You can't get anything out of your Grandie and well, your Gran. So, if we could see the microfiche from the newspaper reports—we'd have a better picture. The council library wasn't any use, they've updated their systems. At least that what the prissy woman at the desk said. Bet she doesn't know what we were talking about. Two, we haven't been able to get into the school systems because Mrs Floozy Turpin says we're not allowed to use the only computer that has the newspaper databases. It's off limits. Three, the school has no security system for the library—it's separate from the school buildings. Four...'

'Hang on, Hang on,' yelped Emma. 'Are you thinking what I think you're thinking? I thought we were going to try and get in there in our lunch hour and look then. We can't go now!'

Jenna waggled her eyebrows.

Ebony paled. 'We can't get in, you twit.'

'But we could...'

'Yeah right. Have you got a lock-picking kit in your backpack? Honestly, Jenna.'

'Don't knock it until you hear me out.' Jenna raised her hands.

'Do you have to do that counting thing, it's really annoying.'

'It helps me think. Don't interrupt. One, it's Turpin's night at the bowling alley in Eiredale. Two, her husband is at the council meeting—they go on for hours. Three, she never locks the house and keeps the keys in the sunroom at the back on a hook.'

'Good grief, you've really thought this through. How did you know that?'

'Jack had to drop something off from Helena and she invited us in. Flirted like mad with Dad, like she does with *everyone*. Thinks that chasm of cleavage is a lure to any man. Dad says...'

'You've started to call him Dad, what's with that?'

181

'Have I? I hadn't noticed. Don't change the subject—you're not paying attention.'

'Well, you certainly *pay attention* enough for both of us,' muttered Emma. 'Sure you don't want to follow in your dad's footsteps?'

Jenna's eyes glinted, sensing a change in Emma's attitude. 'All we have to do is get the key from Mrs Turpin's house, open the library and have a look. We'd be back before anyone even noticed.'

'But...' said Emma, and then when a single clear objection didn't surface she smiled and said, 'What are we waiting for? Dad won't notice—he's a bit high on painkillers after the doc set his leg. Was snoring like a chainsaw when I left to walk down here.'

'Painkillers? Your dad's leg? What the hell happened? You didn't tell me about this.'

'It's a long story...'

'I can't wait,' said Jenna.

Silently as thieves the girls retrieved their bicycles from the front of the house. The cul-de-sac was dark. There was a flickering light in the lounge room. A dog barked. Ebony flinched. She wasn't cut out for this caper. A pulse throbbed in her throat.

The girls rode swiftly, taking back roads. When they arrived at 48 Generation Drive there was a soft glow in the front room.

'Someone's home. We'll have to go back and come another time,' said Ebony.

'She always leaves that on,' said Jenna.

'You've really cased the joint, haven't you?'

'Thanks for noticing.'

'Can't we just check if there's a car in the garage?' asked Emma.

'Their garage has no windows. Anyway it doesn't matter. There's a sunroom at the back. It's kind of separate to the house. We won't even be inside. Come on!'

The girls crept to the back of the house. Emma could hear her heart thumping in her ears.

'Jenna, your backpack's rattling. What did you bring?'

Jenna held a finger up to her lips.

Huddled behind several camellia bushes the girls paused. Emma threw Jenna a "what now" look, but Jenna only touched the side of her nose. Grabbing Emma's hand, she tiptoed onto the back porch. Holding the screen door handle, she slipped it open. It gave a small squeak of protest that made Emma jump.

Slowly turning the doorknob to the old timber door, Jenna eased it open. Beckoning to Emma, she held the door ajar. Emma padded across the last few feet to the door and slid inside. Jenna's face was intense in the half-light. She produced a tiny torch the size of a peanut. They were alone in the sunroom. With a pinpoint of light, she scanned the back wall. With a gentle 'Aha' she flipped a set of keys off the hook and held them aloft in triumph.

'What the bloody hell!'

The back door to the house flew open. Light flooded the sunroom. Emma screamed. Jenna shaded her eyes.

A shirtless Clive Brisley was holding a baseball bat in one hand while the other hand struggled with the fly on his trousers.

An arresting moment

'They tell me you're good with the cranky patients. Is that why you're here?' asked Brady, peering through a small opening in the door so he could face Emma.

His left leg was encased in a cumbersome walking boot. The chatty physiotherapist at the outpatient's department had assured him he'd be 'as good as new in a few weeks, six at the most'. She'd then given him a pair of crutches to 'get him started, just bring them back in a week or two. They're a hospital loan—free of course.'

He winced as the setting sun shone brightly behind her, giving her a radiant glow. She was in her nurses' uniform. He had been longing to see her with an ache he couldn't describe, but not like this. He inched the door open a fraction.

'Ouch!' The boot connected with the door.

One of his crutches fell to the floor with a thud.

'Sod it!'

Brady tried to retrieve it, but couldn't reach. He looked up at Emma.

'What's that?'

'One of my crutches. The flake I saw at the hospital gave them to me. I'd never have picked her for having a school education, much less a degree. Is she qualified? She looks all of fourteen.'

'Actually, she's in her thirties and she's a competent physio according to her résumé. Don't judge a book by its cover. I'm just here to check on you.'

'Oh, well, that's, er, bother! I don't want to be your patient. It's a huge impediment to a man falling for a woman to be seen as a complete wreck. And also grubby and cranky.'

'Well, you're stuck with me. Are you going to leave me here by the...What *is* that thing? A swan or a goose?' asked Emma, tripping on a clay object of dubious species.

'Neither. It's a duck,' said Brady. 'Ebony made it for me.'

'Is that what you tripped over when you broke your leg?'

Brady coloured. 'No. I bought a new bike. It appears I've forgotten how to ride.'

'Oh. How does Ebony feel about that?'

'She wasn't there when I...er, fell off. Steve took me to the hospital. Anyway, I don't want to talk about it. The wretched child just laughed at me, phoned for pizza and went off to Jenna's.'

'Well, if you open the door properly.'

'I can't.'

Emma smiled. 'Oh? Being difficult, are we?'

'No, *we* are not!'

'Just you then.'

Brady moaned. 'My leg...well, this bally boot thing, is wedged against the door.'

'That's a problem then,' said Emma.

'You don't have to look so pleased.'

'Oh, but I do.' Emma grinned. 'Is the back door unlocked?'

'Yes.'

'Okay,' said Emma, 'I'll come around that way.'

Brady moaned. The worst of it was that he could be like this for weeks. When he'd worked at the youth centre he'd seen dozens of guys with drug-related injuries deftly weaving around on crutches. He had a new respect for their skills. Even with the help of the physio, he was mediocre at best.

Emma padded into the room. Brady sighed. She looked like sunshine and smelled of woodlands. She picked up the wayward crutch, led him to the sofa and helped him lower into its plush brown softness. 'Brady! Why do you have crutches as well as the boot?'

'How should I know? You mean I don't need the rotten things?'

'Probably not. It's called a *walking boot* for good reason. Why don't you lean on me and try without the crutches?'

'Great,' said Brady, 'just great!'

Her outstretched arm was more than he could resist. He took her hand and threw his arm around her shoulder.

'Ouch!' Emma yelped at his tight grip.

'Sorry,' he said, grinning wickedly.

'You can put your full weight on the boot. You can't do any more damage. What did you break anyway?'

Brady hesitated. 'My toe.'

Emma giggled uncontrollably.

'I don't appreciate that response,' he said, 'they told me it was a rare injury—it's called a ballet fracture.'

Emma only laughed harder. 'Oh, Misery Guts, what am I going to do with you?'

Brady stomped across the room.

'Brady! You walked without the crutches!...and me.'

Brady looked down and grinned like a schoolboy. 'Well, what do you know? That daft physio.'

Emma shook her head. 'She's completely dippy.'

'Come and sit with me.' Brady sat and patted the lounge chair beside him. 'Anyway, on another note, thanks for helping Dad—he's thrilled with the companion dog, they've called her Misty. She follows Mum everywhere. Dotes on her. I think she actually calms Mum down.'

'You're welcome.' Emma stood.

'You're leaving?' Brady blurted, instantly regretting

the desperate tone in his voice.

'No, I'm not leaving. I'm going to make us a cup of tea and sit you on the back porch for some fresh air.' Emma leaned across him to pick up his empty coffee mug.

Brady drew in a ragged breath. Struggling for words to cover his reaction, he said, 'I look a right wreck.'

'You do indeed. I can't believe you fell off a pushbike. What were you thinking?'

'Arrggh. I'll never live this down. I bought it to go riding with Ebony. I wanted something to enjoy together. I hardly see her anymore and...'

Emma dissolved into a fit of laughter.

'It's not that funny! Oh, stop,' he moaned. 'Don't you think I've had enough from Steve and all the teenagers who hang out here?'

Emma put her head down, but her shoulders were shaking.

'Keep that up and I'll punish you. Don't push a man on the edge.'

'What are you going to do?' she gurgled, 'beat me with your...*oh!*'

Brady's mouth possessed hers, his lips demanding, seeking. He drew her closer, lifting her across his body. One hand flung the clip that was holding her hair together while the other roamed her face. When he gently tugged on her bottom lip her response was immediate. Replete with her surrender, he replaced urgency with tenderness, caressing her hair and neck.

'Well, what have we here?' said a voice from behind them.

'Jeez, Steve! Don't you ever knock?'

'No time, old son. Ebony and Jenna are in trouble. They're at the police station. I'll drive you.'

Trouble

All the way home from the Police Station, there was silence in the car. Brady was boiling with frustration, and confused as all hell. Ebony sat in the back, arms crossed defiantly. Steve was uncharacteristically silent. Forcing himself to calm down, Brady rehearsed all the things he would say to Ebony when they got home.

She'd better be taking this seriously. No one else seemed to be. The police officer at the desk was highly amused by Clive Brisley's acute embarrassment and desire to 'put the whole thing down to a youthful prank'. Why the silly git had even apologised for Mrs Turpin panicking and calling the police. His muttered explanation of dropping books off to the librarian who was 'sick and needed them' did nothing but cause smirks on the officers' faces. Smirks they hid carefully behind the Principal's back, while maintaining an astonishing level of nonchalant professionalism.

Jack had merely rolled his eyes and thrown Brady a "what can you do" look, which only increased Brady's ire.

He'd get no help from that quarter. The girls needed sorting out and Jack couldn't even see that there was a problem.

Even Clive Brisley was annoyed by Jack's attitude and threatened to mark his card. Jack's reaction had been to throw his head back laughing and remark, 'I'm not one of your students, Brisley. I'd be worried about my own card if I were you.'

Brady's helplessness was increased by his clumsy immobility. He'd had to rely on Steve for a lift, and Steve had treated the whole episode as a free night's entertainment, along with opening doors for him and treating him like an invalid.

'You're not a nurse's bootlaces, Steve,' he'd muttered.

'Ha. You've had enough nursing for one day,' said Steve, who made a hasty exit on their return home.

Ebony dumped her backpack inside the door.

'What on earth were you thinking, Ebony?'

'I wouldn't expect you to understand. It's too late for lectures and ... punishment. Too late for everything. Don't ask me questions when you brought this on yourself.'

'Don't turn this on me!'

'Why not? The police took you in over a misunderstanding. Is there one rule for you and another for me? You've just assumed, like you always do. You think you know what I'm thinking, but you don't have a clue. You treated me like a...You humiliated me back there. You didn't ask for my side of the story—you just apologised to the policeman as if you were embarrassed by me. Was it the same policeman that picked you up, Dad? Was it? That'd be *choice*.'

'This is different—you were inside the school librarian's house!'

'On her porch!'

'She phoned the police to report a break-in!'

'Well, of course—believe *her* over your own daughter, believe a lying tart who's cheating on her husband. I wouldn't have had to be there if you...'

'If I what? What have I done?' Brady's face was etched with pain.

'It's what you didn't say, Dad,' said Ebony. 'You've avoided all my questions.'

'I was protecting you.'

'That's the single most evasive, self-indulgent sentence in *the history of sentences*—said by everyone who really means "I was protecting myself from the fallout of how you would feel", from the mess the truth would create.'

'You need to remember there are things I don't know. I didn't want to see you hurt. I couldn't trust myself to get it right...'

'You couldn't trust *me*, Dad, *me*. An ugly truth is better than the best-dressed lie.'

'I didn't lie. You have to know that. *Know me.*'

'Silence is the biggest lie of all. You lied. I don't know

if I can forgive that, but not right now. I understand why you couldn't, in the early dark days. I was just a kid, *but later*, later Dad, when you could have been brave enough, honest enough. What's the use of all the heroism in the world, the slaying of corporate dragons, building an empire—when, at the end of the day, you come home to one small person, your own child, and can't say, "Your mother killed herself". I know she was afraid, and, and human, but she was a coward. She left this world by choice. Left us! But hey, she was mentally ill, she had a reason. You're a bigger coward than she ever was!' Ebony trembled with anger.

'My God, I had no idea you felt like this.'

'You could have fixed this. You must have known that one day I would hear the truth whispered, the gossip, the lies—never knowing which was which. Did you expect me to be a robot? Did you honestly think I would never want answers?'

'You didn't ask about the accident. I don't understand. You only had to ask.'

'*Really? Ask?* You didn't want me to. I'm not stupid. You told me nothing, *nothing!*' Tears coursed down Ebony's cheeks. 'I've had to skulk around libraries, newspapers with Jenna, and not with the one I really wanted—my dad.'

'That's what all this is about? The break in? You were trying to find out about your mother?'

'You're unbelievable. Your lack of trust in me is astonishing. Did you think I'd become a bloody nosy parker overnight? Obsessed with fat school Principals and librarians and...affairs? Why couldn't you tell me the truth, Dad? I have to ask, even though you won't have any shadow of a decent answer. Go on, here's your chance. At least tell me why you couldn't talk to your own daughter.'

'I just couldn't.'

'Then I'll tell you why, Dad. You couldn't tell me the truth because you couldn't tell yourself the truth. You couldn't face your own questions. How am I doing so far?'

Brady's face paled.

'I thought so,' said Ebony, wrapping her arms around herself protectively, 'We didn't lose the glue that held us together when Mum died. We lost a pantomime—we never had *real*.'

Brady slumped into the sofa. 'Eb...I...'

'It was so selfish, Dad. Did you ever think I would wonder if I might be like Mum?'

'Like her? What do you mean, like your mother?'

'That I might develop bipolar? That I might want to be prepared for that? That I might want to know why she killed herself. There's a huge difference between sleepwalking and suicide—*God help me*—did you think I slept through all those midnight discussions, those whispered conversations with Nana and Pop Camberwell and Grandie and Grandma, not to mention Uncle Steve?

Either way, sleepwalking or suicide I had so much to lose—if she sleepwalked it might happen to me. If it was suicide, I might...'

'Don't say it.'

'I will say it. It's time for *saying*. How can you begin to understand? You don't have her blood in your veins—but I do! You don't have her genes—but I do!' The words caught in Ebony's throat, coming out hoarsely. She realised she'd been yelling, but she no longer cared. The dam had broken its banks. 'When you think about it, I might have Grandma Betty's genes too, maybe I'll have bipolar, but hey, that's okay—I might get Alzheimer's and forget about it.'

Brady was shocked into silence. He'd never heard his daughter like this, never seen bitterness and sarcasm—not about this. Her cynicism cut like a knife. For the first time he actually wondered if there was a possibility that Ebony might have Scarlett's frail mental state. Then he wondered how he had been so blind that he hadn't thought that these were normal fears. He hadn't allowed himself to consider them, but they were obviously torturing his daughter.

'And that family, the other victims in this, the driver and his family. Living with it every day, the same nightmare.' Angry tears ran down Ebony's cheeks. She rubbed at them with the long ends of her hoodie sleeves. 'Do you even know their names? Have you ever thought of them? Just once. Not even when you tried to hold the guy that killed those men in the car? When you saw him beating his chest and tearing out his hair. I thought people made that stuff up, but he was out of his mind. In hell.'

'I held you. I've tried.'

'But you didn't talk about it, *like you never talk about anything.* It's like you're watching life instead of living it. Something else died when Mum did. A part of you, a part of us.' Ebony slumped exhausted against the door jamb.

'We could have talked. You didn't have to act out.'

'Oh, that's rich. The old 'knock on my door anytime' policy. It's rubbish. There are doors that should always be open. Did you really expect me to be the one to start the important conversations? And you talk about acting out as if I'm some uncontrollable delinquent.'

Brady's head fell forward into his hands.

Ebony picked up her backpack, swinging open the screen door.

'I'm leaving—don't look for me. I would stay with Jenna, but she's probably getting the blame for my 'quest'. Right now, I don't want to see you. You had so many chances to make this right. One conversation, once in three and a half years...*just one.'*

The door slammed.

'*Ebony!*' Brady cried, his face contorted.

Losing

'I'm losing her, Steve.'

'You're overreacting, Brady. She's just at Jim's, cooling off. He phoned to let you know where she was before you could phone every police station and hospital in a hundred kilometre radius.' Steve took in Brady's anxious face.

'Well, nearly in time...'

'You didn't?'

'I did.'

'Who?'

'Jenna.'

'Well, at least you didn't make a complete dill of yourself. Again.' Steve helped himself to a beer from the fridge, closed the door, then opened it and brought one to Brady. Brady shook his head. 'It's medicinal, Brady. You seriously need to chill.'

'I'm stuffing this up, aren't I?'

'Only a bit. And only because you're making everything too important. Ebony can't be your whole existence. She'll grow up and leave. It's too much pressure on a kid. Any kid.'

'I should know that better than anyone.'

'Really? Let's go to the lounge room. It's getting chilly.'

The embers flared under Brady's care, as he knelt and added first kindling and then larger pieces of timber with deft hands. He took his time, stoking the coals, positioning the wood.

'I hate to admit it Steve, but you're right. I'm doing the same thing I hated as a kid. I'd better get this right with Ebony or history will repeat itself. I went to Sydney to escape the pressure. I never talked about it with anyone but Scarlett.'

'Tell me about your parents,' Scarlett had said suddenly, regarding him with soft serious eyes. Brady hesitated. She'd ventured on delicate ground. 'Are they happy, do you think?' she asked, twirling her wine glass.

Perhaps it was the late hour, the extra glass of wine or the quiet intent in her voice, but whatever it was, it turned out to be the key to opening Brady up to her.

He leaned back in the chair. 'It's funny how you spend your whole childhood never considering happiness in the context of your parents' marriage,' he said. 'Like you, I'm an only child and I was so much the focus of my parents' lives that I never thought of what made them happy— together or individually. I came along later in life for them, you see. It was as if when I arrived there was only me. Self-absorbed attitude, I know.' Brady gave a hollow laugh.

Scarlett tilted her head towards him.

'It was a shock to hear from my uncle that they hadn't followed their dreams before me. Apparently, I was the dream. The gift they never thought to possess.'

'That's so sweet.'

'You'd think so. But it only made me feel a huge responsibility. If they'd never longed for anything else, that made me everything. I wanted to be part of something, not everything. I wouldn't have minded being the reason for their happiness, but I was the reason for every disagreement, every decision. Well, that's what it felt like—as if I held them together somehow. I used to wonder if I was the only thing they had in common. Stupid really, so many assumptions.' Brady stopped, embarrassed that he'd said so much.

'I don't think that's stupid. What's wrong with that kind of love?' Scarlett kissed his neck. 'You're my...whole world, Brady.'

Brady watched as Steve rose and stoked the fire.

'I loved like that once,' said Steve.

Brady leaned forward, alert. There was a poignant tone to Steve's voice he hadn't heard before.

'Her name was Ingrid, she was Danish. I taught her to

surf. We had so much in common. She loved cars. She wanted to be a mechanic but her parents vetoed that, so she trained as a pharmacist.'

'Wow, did I ever meet her?'

'You might have seen her around, I dunno. You were just a kid.'

'What happened? Did she go back to Denmark?' Brady traced the pattern on the lounge absently, as his uncle's carefree bachelor status slipped.

'She'd been given citizenship a few years before I met her, so she was here to stay. It was no holiday romance, that's for sure.' Steve paused, settling into the lounge with one hand behind his head. 'We did cars up in our spare time.'

'Sounds like the perfect chick.'

'She was perfect for me.'

Brady's brow furrowed, but he waited.

'She went back to Denmark to see her parents. I wanted to go, but she said, "next time". She wanted to tell them about me. The first day she was there she went swimming off the coast.' Steve shuddered, his eyes far away. 'They found her body five days later. I didn't get a chance to say goodbye, couldn't go to the funeral. I didn't get a chance to even grieve for her. Her parents knew nothing about me.'

'God, that's horrible.'

'Yes, it is. But I had that once in a lifetime thing and

I'm grateful.'

'Wow, I don't know what to say, Steve.'

'Don't waste your chances, Brady. Don't waste your heart. And I don't just mean with Ebony.'

Escape

'Well, I must say, Eb, for someone who's run away you haven't run far. You're more like your father than you think.'

Ebony rolled her eyes. At any other time this kind of revelation about her father would have provoked a pleading tone, and a laughing request for more information that would prove Dad was one of the human race. But she was not in a conciliatory mood. Pushing the thought to the back of her mind, she reminded herself to ask her grandfather to tell her the story later.

Jim Harcourt pulled an ancient stone saucepan out of the cupboard. Retrieving the milk from the fridge and the tin of chocolate from the cupboard he switched on the stove.

'Oh Grandie, you remember! I didn't think you had the old saucepan. It's my favourite, it even has the pouring lip, just for hot chocolates for two.'

'I've had to hide it. Your grandmother isn't so good with the stove anymore.'

'I guess you've had to hide a lot of things.'

'You don't know the half.'

They sipped their drinks.

Ebony had flown out the door without a thought or care other than to escape from her father, and perhaps hurt him a little in the process. She waited for her grandfather to ask questions so she could tell him she had no intention of discussing anything to do with her father—now, or ever. But he didn't ask. Which was annoying, really.

She helped Grandie tidy up. He chatted about her grandmother, the woman she had been, and Ebony realised she wasn't the only one who longed for a listening ear. At first she thought it was just a ploy to avoid discussing her sudden windblown arrival, but after an hour or so of cosy conversation she wasn't so sure.

Finally, it was too much.

'I'd really like to talk to you, Grandie. There are things worrying me about Mum. You know, her illness and...well, how she died. Well, lots of stuff. I can't get Dad to listen or talk at all.'

'Did you ask him?'

'I've tried everything.'

'Did you ask?'

'Well, I told him.'

'But did you ask? The way you asked me now?'

'What are you trying to say? What's the difference?'

'All the difference in the world, my pet. There's an ocean between asking and accusation.'

'How do you know? What makes you think that?'

Jim Harcourt eyed her over the top of his spectacles.

'Okay, I didn't exactly ask.'

'I didn't think so. And these questions. What makes you so sure he knows the answers? What if there are no answers? Have you thought of that?'

'That's ridiculous. Sorry, but there's...'

The hall clock chimed the hour.

'Hold that thought, kiddo. I have to check on your Nan.'

Ebony was left gaping into the silence.

When Jim returned Ebony dropped a kiss on his cheek. 'How's Gran?'

'Just fine, kiddo.'

'That's great, Grandie, give her my love.' She patted Misty's golden head and was rewarded with an extended paw.

'You're off then?'

'Yes,' Ebony stood by the door. 'Thanks for the spare bed.' She studied the pattern of the kitchen tiles. 'And thanks for phoning Dad last night and letting him know I was okay. Otherwise he'd have had the entire State police force out.'

Jim viewed his granddaughter through narrowed eyes.

Ebony paused. 'I know you would've done the same.

I'm sorry. 'I'll be late for school. See ya.'

'It's only 8 o'clock. I thought you wanted to talk.'

The door banged.

'Great, talking to myself again.'

Jim rolled his eyes at the swinging door. It was a fair guess that Ebony was rushing out to avoid running into her father.

The Principal's office

'Oh, this should be good,' Jenna leaped to her feet. She and Ebony had just been summoned to Principal Brisley's office by his mouse of a secretary, Ms Bentley.

Ebony's only response was to tremble and hiccup.

'Oh, for God's sake Ebony! Not again. What is it with you and hiccups?' Jenna stood impatiently, hands on hips, in the middle of the corridor crowded with jostling, noisy teens.

Not for the first time, Ebony felt awe at Jenna's apparent indifference to the tide of confusion around her. Unfazed, Jenna looked down at Ebony like a diminutive Lucretia Borgia.

'You didn't hesitate with your father. You gave him a right ticking off. Didn't think you had it in you,' she said. Pausing, she tilted her head. 'Might have been a bit over the top though. He's a good man, you know. You should give him a chance. Men aren't good at words. Trust me. They're not like us.'

Ebony clamped down on a response. She didn't want

to think about her father, the hasty words she'd flung at him. Right now, she didn't want to keep the principal waiting. After all, they had probably already destroyed the poor man's life when they caught him in flagrante. The memory of the look on his face when he caught her and Jenna in the bushes of Mrs Turpin's garden brought fresh shame. She shuddered at the revenge he might take out on them.

Jenna's confidence restored some calm. There was only one person more terrifying than Mr Brisley and that was Jenna. She'd let Jenna do the talking.

Gathering her tattered emotions Ebony stood up to follow Ms Bentley who was clicking her pen as she waited. 'Bloody hiccups,' she murmured. She took a deep breath and held it through at least two hiccups. The technique had worked wonders at the police station.

Ms Bentley kept up a punishing pace, refusing to look back and was far ahead of the girls. Ebony tried to keep up, but Jenna pulled her back.

'Slow down. Don't play into their hands, Eb.'

'Sheesh, I hope we don't get the usual blah about ruining our lives, wasting our parents' money and not performing to our maximum potential,' she said, grateful that her hiccups had subsided.

'Bollocks!' laughed Jenna. 'Nobody talks about maximum potential in a public school. They're too busy just getting through the day. And they *never* mention money. That's one less guilt trip to lay on us. The beauty of free education.'

Ms Bentley ushered them to the two deceptively comfortable-looking chairs outside Mr Brisley's office. Brushing her immaculate coif for an imaginary stray lock of hair she sat down in the small cubicle that was her domain.

'Your hiccups have stopped already,' said Jenna. 'That's an improvement. There's nothing a little breath-holding and diversional therapy can't fix.'

Ebony wasn't so sure, but she declined to comment. She had already been shocked by Jenna's admission that she'd held her breath until she turned blue when she was a toddler.

'I hope he doesn't take too long,' said Ebony, always ready to worry about timetables and lateness. She twisted the hem of her uniform. 'We'll be late for History.'

'Oh no. He'll be ages,' said Jenna.

Ebony turned confused eyes to her friend.

'Don't you get it Eb? *This* is the punishment—the waiting. We are supposed to sit here and churn about what we have done, feel deeply sorry and worry about the consequences. Which is all a great waste of time because they can't actually do anything to us. Brisley just wants us to stew.'

This brave speech only served to further shock Ebony.

'Anyway,' continued Jenna, 'he won't even bring the

subject of our adventure up. He'll be too embarrassed. He'll try and throw his weight around to scare us into silence. He has more to lose than us. He won't want it getting out about his sordid affair.'

'Ooh, that's blackmail,' said Ebony.

'Not if we don't say it, it isn't.'

'With you around I'm getting more of an education in the corridors than the classroom,' said Ebony. Plastering a smile on her face that she hoped conveyed both respect and penitence she stood as Mr Brisley thrust his considerable bulk into the small foyer.

'Come in girls,' he said cheerily.

Jenna winked at Ebony. 'We are deeply sorry for causing you embarrassment and wish to assure you that it will never happen again,' she said, spreading her hands expansively.

Ebony had a vision of Jenna in parliament appealing for the underdog—or on the stage—which was pretty much the same thing.

Clive Brisley winced. The cheek of the girl. He'd been outplayed by a teenage girl with the battle skills of Alexander the Great. The little wretch was leaning forward and meeting his gaze with calm audacity. Her words may have said sorry. However, her eyes said anything but. Seeking to regain some control, he leaned forward to match her and smiled the smile that usually earned him victory at the P & C meetings. With a nonchalant wave of his hand he dismissed the matter. 'That's not why I wanted to see you. I know that was just a prank. You girls would never make anything out of an afterhours visit to a staff member to drop off a book.'

Jenna shot Ebony a "what did I tell you look".

Brisley hesitated, wondering why schools had ever stopped corporal punishment. 'I want to ask you both to take on the important role of school prefects.'

Ebony sat stunned, but Jenna's equanimity was unperturbed. She manufactured a sincere face designed to convey that she was giving the matter her complete attention.

Brisley filled in the silence with a wordy description of how the prefect system worked at his school, what would be expected of them, placing emphasis on the high honour he was bestowing.

At the end of his speech Jenna said, 'that's very gratifying, Mr Brisley. Although, speaking for myself, I will have to decline. There doesn't seem to be much scope to formulate positive change and raise student issues effectively.'

Brisley was furious. The school reports that accompanied Jenna had not thoroughly prepared him for this feisty nuisance of a girl.

'But thanks for thinking of us,' she added.

Ebony felt the surge of an unfamiliar emotion. 'Yes, Mr Brisley. We are both committed to social change and engagement, and where better to start than right here at school. As you said last week in general assembly, this is the Petrie dish for future academic and social growth.'

It was Jenna's turn to be shocked.

Brisley stiffened. That's all I need, he thought, apparently submissive Miss Bloody Brain Box to join the rank and file. He'd been fostering hopes of school glory through Ebony. He'd enjoyed giving that rousing talk in general assembly, but was less than impressed to have it thrown back in his face. With a mumbling attempt at regaining his composure he ushered them out the door and collapsed back in his chair.

'Ms Bentley! Have you any Panadol?' he roared. He was rewarded with the sound of the phone hitting the floor, then a scuffling noise as his secretary went through her desk drawers.

Jenna and Ebony ran giggling towards the humanities block. The heady feeling of power and success was so unfamiliar to Ebony that she accidentally sent a surly look at Miss Abbott, the gym teacher. Miss Abbott, who was universally liked by students and staff, was so shocked by this reaction from the usually compliant Ebony that she ploughed into the door of the classroom she was entering.

Ebony felt immediately remorseful.

Jenna rolled her eyes in horror. 'Don't let power go to your head Eb.'

'Oh dear.'

'But especially don't go back to door mouse or I will have to slap you out of it.'

'I feel dreadful. I'll have to go and be nice to Miss Abbott later.'

'No! That's the worst thing you can do. That only makes them think you're a hormonally neurotic teenager. Better to pretend it never happened. Just explaining things only confuses them. They're only teachers, after all.'

This scathing indictment silenced Ebony, but she secretly planned to go back and make it up to Miss Abbott. In future she would be careful who received poisonous glares.

They reached the door of the History class. 'Oh dear, we're late,' said Ebony.

'You worry too much, Eb. It's only Mangret, he must be filling in.'

'Oh no, what's he like? I haven't had him before.'

'He's a doddle. Never raises his voice. He's the school Welfare Officer. Shush, we're here.'

Ebony's intention of slipping unnoticed into the history class was foiled by Jenna saying loudly, 'Sorry sir, sorry to be late Mr Mangret. Won't happen again, sir.'

Mr Neville Mangret didn't even look up. Weary of the world and teenagers in particular Mr Mangret continued to drone on as he read the textbook aloud. He didn't even notice the unfamiliar title of "sir". The other students called him Mangy and he had not once protested, simply accepting the dreadful shortening of his name as his lot in an already tedious life. Reading the textbook out loud was the perfect excuse to never look up at the class.

The only disciplinary technique on his side was a slightly odd look he unknowingly gave the students. The fact that he didn't care what they thought was a lethal combination and had the effect of making the students feel it was a waste of time to target him.

At the end of the class Neville Mangret stood and handed out homework sheets. As he walked down the aisles of desks he gave each student a brief nod. When he came to Ebony's desk, he hesitated. She looked up and smiled. There was something familiar about the girl.

The moment passed and he moved on.

Tell me about you

'Brady, you look frightful.' Emma sat down at the kitchen table in the cottage.

'Gee, thanks,' said Brady. 'Ebony didn't come home last night.'

'Oh, no. Where did she go?'

'To Dad's. He phoned.'

'Bit unimaginative,' said Emma. 'That shows she wasn't too serious. She's a bit too sensible to go far. Can I get you a cuppa?'

'No thanks, you make rubbish coffee. I'll do it. I'm getting pretty good with this boot. Would you like a mocha?'

'Yes, please,' she said, 'especially if you're making gourmet coffee with that complicated machine. I haven't worked mine out yet.'

'Looks like I have a permanent job.' He threw Emma a knowing look and deftly started the coffee machine. The hiss of steam and the aroma filled the room.

'Wow, that's great, Brady. Are you going in to work

today?'

'No I have paperwork to do at home. That's the great thing about the job. I thought I'd be here for Ebony but she went to school from Dad's.'

'Well, that's good. She'll come round, she's a great kid.' Emma accepted the steaming mug.

They sat in silence, sipping their coffees, each lost in their own thoughts.

'Did she give you any explanation about last night?'

'Nothing that made sense. I've never seen her so upset. She blamed me.' Brady winced as he stretched his leg.

'You're in pain, Brady. Have you taken your medication?'

'I dunno. No, not since last night. I forgot.'

'Where is it? I'll get it for you and we can sit in the lounge room. Come on, accept a little TLC.'

Brady pointed wearily at the kitchen bench. Emma gave him a shooing motion, and he obediently limped to the lounge room and slumped into the sofa.

'Here you are. Take two. You have a broken foot Brady, you need to remember to take them. A fracture in the joint is painful.'

'Tell me about it.' Brady took the pills and rested his head on the back of the sofa. Emma shifted the ottoman closer and insisted he rest his leg. She put some soft music on, told him to relax and massaged his neck.

'I just...'

'Shh, Brady, let my hands do their magic, and give the pills a chance to work. Then we'll talk.'

Brady's breathing slowed. 'That's wonderful. Where'd you learn that?' he murmured.

While she kneaded the muscles of his neck, Emma felt the tension leave his body. His eyes closed. She kicked her shoes off and sat beside him. His eyes drifted open and he reached out an arm to draw her closer. She leaned into his body, enjoying the warmth of his embrace. Then she heard gentle snoring. She shifted in his arms and his arm tightened around her. Smiling, she gave into the serenity of the moment and leaned her head on his shoulder.

She thought she would get up and tidy the place after Brady was deeply asleep. The house was littered with pizza boxes and chip packets. He'd said Steve had brought groceries, but it seemed Steve's idea of the essentials was typical bachelor fare.

The snoring grew louder. Emma found herself reluctant to move. Brady's grip hadn't lessened, even in sleep. She let her eyelids flutter shut, and drifted with him.

The phone jarred them awake. Emma leapt up, grabbed the handset and gave it to Brady. He stared at it as if it was an alien object and when he spoke his voice was hoarse. 'Dad? Sure, come on over. Emma's here too. Okay, great, you'd like to talk to her too? No worries. The back door's open.'

Emma eyed the room.

'Don't tidy up,' said Brady.

'I wasn't going to. You're beyond help.'

'Gee, thanks.'

'I have a list of good domestic cleaners,' said Emma smiling.

'Aren't you just a helpful little thing. You could just give me referrals on all kinds of services couldn't you?'

'Might not be a bad idea, son,' said Jim, stepping into the room. 'Doesn't hurt to accept help.' Jim sat on the single sofa opposite.

'Well, if that isn't the pot calling the kettle black,' said Brady, scowling.

'This kettle is turning over a new leaf, son.'

'Mixing your metaphors, Dad. What new leaf?'

'I need help.'

Brady leaned forward. 'What's wrong Dad?'

Jim sighed. 'It's your mother. Apparently, she's been phoning some woman late at night for the past few months asking for her sister, Deidre. This woman has Deidre's old phone number.'

'But Aunt Deidre died years ago. How has Mum managed to phone without you hearing her?'

'I don't know. I must sleep through it. I'm so weary. Anyway, I'm so sorry for this poor woman. I don't know what to do. I can't watch Betty every minute of the day, and I'd hate to hide the phone.'

'Can you get a code for it?' asked Brady. 'So she can't ring long distance?'

'I'd hate to do that, she sometimes manages it really well, and phones friends.'

'I think there is an easier way,' said Emma. Both men turned to her. 'If you could speak to this woman, she could get her phone company to block your number. That way she won't get any more calls. Do you have the number?'

'Yes, I do.' Jim pulled out a note. 'She phoned this morning, she was quite upset. She thought Betty was phoning from a nursing home, or hostel of some sort and wanted to speak to the supervisor to make the calls stop. I was so embarrassed.'

'Would you like me to phone her and explain what she can do,' asked Emma. 'I've had to do it for clients.'

'Would you? That would be wonderful, Emma. Thanks.' Jim handed Emma the sheet and she took it into the kitchen.

'She's a gem, that girl,' said Jim.

Brady smiled. 'The best.'

'Hmm.' Jim pursed his lips.

'I love her, Dad.'

'Then there's hope for you yet.' Jim smiled. 'I will be taking her advice. Looking into things. Day care, and maybe a specialist.'

'I'll come with you if you like, Dad. Let me be there for

you. I came home for a reason. You and Mum are part of that reason.'

Jim took out a handkerchief and wiped his eyes. 'Thanks son. Appreciate it.'

Emma padded back into the room. 'It's all sorted, Jim.' She sat beside Brady. Brady put his arm around her. 'How was Ebony this morning Dad? She was really mad with me.'

'She went off to school okay. She's a teenager, son.'

'Ebony is usually so calm, Brady. It's not like her to yell, she's a pretty chill kid really. I've often thought she was a lot like you,' said Emma.

'I don't think she'd like the comparison, but then...' Brady stopped short. 'She said she was worried about being like her mother. And a whole lot of other stuff.'

'She's angry, son. You two need to talk. Scarlett's death left so many questions, the way she died. Ebony has questions. She doesn't understand.'

'Yeah,' said Brady, 'that's pretty much the gist of what she said. It's been brewing to a head. I should have seen this coming. I mean, things had changed, but I had no idea what to do. I thought having more time with her would help.'

'It's only natural that she would worry about having bipolar, she's at that age. It would hang over her head. I don't know the circumstances or how her mother handled it, but kids in that situation often end up with a carer role. They take on housework and meals, cover up for the parent to protect the family.'

'Oh dear. That makes sense. Sometimes Scarlett would stay in bed for days. She hated taking her meds.'

'Children can often see themselves as guardians, and try to fill the gaps, check up on the medications, get meals. Makes it hard for them to have friends.' Emma touched Brady's arm. 'They hold it all in.'

'And now she wants to talk,' said Brady. 'Of course. That's why she's worried about the accident. She's convinced her mother committed suicide. I didn't know what to say. I have my own questions. Oh God, what a mess.' Brady dropped his head into his hands. 'I didn't want to face any of this. I've been so bloody afraid to lose Ebony too.'

'That's seems to be about the crux of it, son,' said Jim.

'You only lose people who don't want to communicate,' said Emma, lifting Brady's chin. 'And it's you she wants to talk to Brady. That's huge.'

'It is, isn't it? She said she shouldn't have to be roaming all over town with Jenna looking for answers when it should be me.'

'She couldn't make it much plainer, son.'

'But that doesn't explain last night.'

'It might. They might have been after the library key!' said Jim. 'Sheila Turpin is the librarian and keeps the keys on the porch. Her husband, Basil's been on to her for ages about the safety of it. Maybe she keeps the keys there for Brisley. He seems a regular visitor.'

'Well, the whole fiasco is starting to make some sense,' said Brady. I need to sit down and talk to her. Let her know she can ask anything.'

'Sounds like a plan, son.' Jim stood to leave. 'Anyway Emma, when you've got time I'd like to set up some activities and interventions for Betty.'

'That will require you to think of some respite for yourself, Jim.' Emma walked with him to the door.

'Bye Dad.'

'How do you feel, Brady? You had quite a nap.'

'Better thanks. You realise that's the second time we've slept together.'

Emma laughed.

'Thanks for everything, Emma.'

'Happy to help.'

'You could take my mind off things.'

Emma wagged a warning finger at him. 'That would depend.'

'Tell me about you. The story of Emma.'

'Oh. *Really?*'

'You were expecting something else?' Brady grinned. He relaxed back into the chair. 'I'm all ears.'

'Okay then, the short version, Brady.'

'Oh, well, if it's the short version, how can a man

refuse? You know how we men hate sagas.'

'You're such a bloke, Brady.'

Brady sat patiently, his face earnest.

Emma sighed. 'I was engaged. I guess you know that. Ben was in the Army.'

'He was the Creighton boy, wasn't he? Killed in action?'

'Training exercises actually.'

'Oh right.'

'Well, the upshot is, he was exciting, a real risk taker. Adrenaline junkie. It was one long adventure to be with him.'

'I heard he was a live wire.'

'It was more than that. He courted danger.'

'Dead opposite of me.' Brady frowned.

'When I came through the grief of losing him, I realised I didn't like that side of him. I really wonder now if we'd have made the distance. I've seen more of life— pain does that. Opens your eyes to things you don't want to face.'

'He was young.'

'I'm not sure if he would ever have settled down, and I desperately wanted—need that.' Emma paused, swilling the remains of her coffee.

'I like the use of the present tense.' Brady leaned forward and took her hand. 'You *need* that. You know what that means, don't you?'

223

'What does it mean, Brady?'

'You need someone like me.'

'Not someone *like* you, sweet man,' Emma said, gently brushing her lips across his. 'Someone who *is* you.'

Brady rose quickly and crushed her to him. He whispered her name while he kissed her neck.

'I love you, Brady Harcourt. You're all the things I need. I'm not saying you're perfect, but the man you are, well, that's what I see and want in my life.'

'I want that in writing,' he said.

With but a heartbeat later and an inch to breach, they were kissing. Neither of them had expected this, but neither was surprised. It was the most natural thing in the world.

His lips were full and supple, gently tasting her sweetness.

It was unlike any other kiss Emma had known. He was giving, not taking; leaving her to set the pace. Putting her in complete control, deliberately taking his time. This released a freedom in Emma that gave her a new kind of safety. *I could do this forever,* she thought.

Kissing Ben had always seemed like a collision, a precursor to something else, but with Brady, the kiss was the destination. He was savouring, creating, nurturing. Sliding her arms up his chest and linking her hands behind his head, Emma surrendered completely. This was no grab in the dark, no push or pull. No demand or expectation. It was a moment of sharing.

As they kissed, they talked. As their tongues met and meshed, plunging the sweetness of the other, their words connected their souls.

'My God, you smell wonderful,' said Emma.

Brady covered her mouth, deepening the kiss, then retreating to gentle gliding across her lips. Stronger, softer. Yin and Yang.

'How has someone as sweet as you been so alone?' he whispered.

Emma wondered how they were able to speak without the kiss ending, the connection unbroken. 'I'm hiding,' she said, wondering how the truth had escaped her lips when it hadn't even been recognised by her mind.

His tongue sought her again. 'You shouldn't.'

His arms were wrapped around her, neither drawing her closer, nor releasing her. His hands were linked behind the small of her back. They didn't wander or roam. There was no hurry. This was passion of a different kind.

'I have wanted this for so long,' he said.

Emma slid her tongue along the length of his bottom lip, wondering at her audacity. Security—that was it, the word to describe the feeling. Delighting in the moment she rejoiced that passion had words, and not just mindless lust. She could control this, it was okay. It was just a kiss. Okay, lots of kisses that seemed like one long kiss.

'Are you okay?' he asked.

'Okay doesn't begin to describe it.' Emma's mouth never left his.

'I shouldn't.'

'You should,' she said.

'Where have you been, where has your soul been before me?'

'I don't know.'

The warmth of his body seeped through her, and still there was no urgency from him. Continuing his worship of her mouth, Brady caressed her back. Then, deepening the kiss he pulled her closer.

Emma was no innocent, but still she thought this was just a moment. It wouldn't sear her heart. She could savour, then forget.

Minutes passed. The world retreated. There was no other sound but their soft words and the melding of their lips, gently claiming.

'You are really good at this aren't you,' he said.

'If you say so.'

With delicate long strokes Brady caressed her back. 'Is your heart still beating?'

'Hmm? I'm not dead,' she laughed.

'So you're alive.'

'Deliciously.' She sighed.

Without being aware Emma's response was increasing. And yet Brady didn't advance or retreat.

Feeling safer, she touched his face, the stubble, and the smooth. Manly. She revelled in the joy of being in the arms of a man. This man. Barely aware in a hidden corner of her mind that this man was the only one who could move her this way. Gently, exquisitely.

She couldn't contemplate the kiss ending, but neither could she imagine the fire of passion intruding. Until he took both hands and, lightly touching her neck he moved them slowly through her hair, sending electric sparks through her body. She shuddered. Her breathing was uneven now and with a flash she knew she was undone.

Brady's breathing changed too, it was deeper, hungrier.

'You are too lovely,' he murmured, his voice altered. One hand moved to cup the curve of her derriere as he gathered her closer.

It was then she knew he was undone too. This was so much more than a kiss.

'How can my lips ever leave yours?' he rasped gently, lifting the phone off the hook.

Her arms tightened around him. 'They shouldn't.'

Brady blew in her ear. 'Did you lock the door?'

Bridge

Ebony threw pebbles at the ocean. The sea lapped gently on the shore. The zephyrs of spring were surrendering to summer. She and her father had formed an awkward truce of sorts. By tacit agreement they only spoke of the everyday things, each dancing around the tension of the previous weeks.

When she'd come home from school after staying with Grandie, he'd seemed different, tentative. 'I'm here,' he'd said, 'if you want to...talk. You know. About anything.' But was he ready, really? Was he prepared to tackle the tough questions?

She sighed. There was only one way to find out. Dropping the handful of pebbles, Ebony walked along the crooked wire and timber fence that reminded her of an old man with random teeth missing—and went home.

'Hey Eb.' Brady stood awkwardly in the kitchen with his hands in his pockets. 'How was your day?'

'Good.'

'Oh, that's great, sweetheart.'

228

'Dad, do you think you could help me with my economics assignment. You know how useless I am with numbers.'

Brady picked a box up from the floor and placed it on the kitchen table. 'Sure, if you like. But I thought we could work on this.'

Ebony's eyes brightened. 'Is that what I think it is?'

'Yes, Eb. It's the box of your mother's things. I thought we could go through it. You're right. I didn't want to face the past, so I held back from you. I'm sorry, I want to change that. There's stuff I don't know, but we'll work it out together.'

'Oh, Dad! I love you. I'm so sorry for what I said. I hate being angry with you.'

'I love you too, kiddo.'

'I've got a few things too, Dad. I found them in the box of photos of Mum. You know, the ones we had the fight over. I wanted to ask, but...' Ebony went to her room and brought out the box.

Brady paled when he saw the jewellery pouch. 'Oh God, I've almost forgotten about that ring. The first time I saw it was when I went to the morgue to identify your mother.' Tears streamed down his face and Ebony wrapped her arms around him.

'Oh, Dad, how awful!'

'Grandie took the call. I've never talked about it, Eb, but I'm glad it's out in the open now. We can look for answers together.'

Heads bent together they sorted through the small memory box. Inside an envelope there was a variety of pieces of paper, some were scrawled shopping lists and some were receipts. There were paper clips, neatly folded lolly wrappers and hairpins.

'That's Mum, all right. She often had weird stuff and notes in funny places. Sometimes there'd be pills or pages from magazines.'

'I didn't know that.'

'I didn't want to worry you. I wanted to...'

'Protect me,' said Brady with a wry smile.

'I'm such a hypocrite. Sorry, Dad.'

'No more apologies, okay?'

'Okay.'

While they sorted and picked up each new object they shared the fears they had about Scarlett. The way they had each tried to cover and hide the symptoms of her illness. How they had kept things from everyone, but mainly each other. Admitting how hard it had been, each realised how little they knew of the other's angst.

They found Ebony's earliest drawings, her love poems to her mother. They laughed over her scribbled Mother's Day cards.

'Do you think she killed herself, Dad?'

'I really don't think so, Eb. I know how it all looks, but

she'd been through tough times before.'

'I found this.' Ebony showed Brady the scholarship letter.

Brady read it quietly. 'She didn't tell me about this. Wow, that's fabulous.'

'She would have been happy about it, wouldn't she?' asked Ebony. 'It's a good thing, right?'

'Well. When your mother was manic she felt she could do anything, but sometimes she was riddled with self-doubt. It doesn't surprise me that she hadn't mentioned it. She'd have wanted to sort it out first. She was in some art classes when we were here on holiday for the summer months when she died. Some famous artist. She didn't tell me his name, but she had new inspiration.'

'There can't be too many private art tutors in the area, can there?' asked Ebony.

'You'd be surprised. There are quite a few, it's a very arty area.'

'So you tried to find out?'

'I looked in the yellow pages and the newspapers and phoned a few, but it was so hard. I didn't know what to say, you know? And I didn't want to get in the way of the police investigation.'

'I see.'

They were silent when they found a brown paper bag with a bundle of prescriptions and pharmacy bags of medications.

'Why didn't she take her medication, Dad?'

'I never understood it. I could never cope with the highs and the black dog that shadowed her at times, so I never understood why.'

'Did you ask her?'

'Yes, often.'

'What did she say?'

'That they stopped her being herself. That they made her numb, made her someone else,' Brady said.

'But, lots of people have bipolar. They can't all be like that. Did the doctors explain it to you?'

'It was really hard to get them to talk to me sometimes. And in the last few years your mother wouldn't talk about any of it. They found no traces of medication in her system in the Pathology reports after she died, but there were current prescriptions. She always had those. She hardly ever filled them, and when she did she rarely took them.'

'This script is just a week before she died, Dad,' Ebony said showing him the date on the script.

'I never noticed that. She must've seen a doctor up here.'

Brady stretched,

Well, we've looked at the paperwork. There are so many receipts, it's like she collected them, even for pencils. Bit obsessive really. There isn't one for the ring, none from a jeweller?'

'No, I couldn't find one.'

Brady laughed. 'I thought of putting an ad in the paper to find out, but what could I say? "The husband of recently deceased Scarlett Harcourt wishes to know where she obtained a ruby ring." I would've looked like a complete nutter.'

'I see what you mean. That's going to be a tough. Is it important?'

'Well, kind of,' said Brady. 'It's just...'

'You wondered if she was having an affair?'

'That was one possibility, and I was afraid of what I'd find out. So I didn't do any more than visit one jeweller. He took one look at me, and I felt, well, grubby.' Brady shrugged.

'I understand that,' said Ebony.

'I can't believe we're talking about this.'

'Well, it would have been really hard on you, Dad. I can see that now. And there were so many things you couldn't lay on a twelve-year-old, I get that.'

'But I could have...'

'No more apologies, remember?'

'Sure.' Brady smiled.

Ebony reached over and kissed his cheek. 'I was hoping there'd be a journal, or a diary. Something with her thoughts, her writing.'

'She was encouraged to keep a journal by the psychologists, but I don't think she did. I never asked.'

'I'd just like something with her writing on it. I'd settle for her name on the flyleaf of a book.'

'She always said she communicated through her art. I don't even…wait a minute. I have one letter from her. One she wrote on our honeymoon.'

'Oh. But that's private.'

'Actually, it's okay. I'll get it. It's lovely, she wouldn't mind.' Brady retrieved the letter from his room and handed it to Ebony.

Ebony's hands trembled as she unfolded the letter. She looked to him for final reassurance, then read it. 'That's beautiful, Dad. Straight from the heart. I'll look at her paintings in a new way now.'

Brady smiled. 'I want you to talk to someone about the genetic side, if you're willing. By yourself, or whatever.'

'I'd like to talk to Emma.' Ebony's smile was shy.

'You really like her don't you.'

'Not as much as you do, Dad.'

'About that…'

'Now, that's one thing I don't want to hear about. Other than you're madly in love, want to get married and have another kid, brother or sister will do. But, I'm not fussed about hearing details. That would be too too weird.'

'You shock me!'

'Well, she's so good for you. If you don't get a move on and ask her, I will,' said Ebony. 'You don't know how much I've been hoping you'd wake up to yourself.'

'Okay, okay. I thought you'd been dabbling in a bit of matchmaking, but I'm perfectly capable of working that out myself. I don't want an image of you on one knee to the woman I love. I can man up to that question!'

'Glad to hear it.'

'You don't know how happy I am to have your blessing, Eb.'

'You don't mean to tell me that's what you were waiting for?'

'Well, kind of.'

'Good grief, Dad.'

Brady shrugged.

'Can I be your best man?' Ebony tilted her head, mischief lighting her eyes.

'Sure. I'll hire a coat and tails for you.'

'Don't tempt me, Dad. I'd look great in a morning suit. When are you going to ask her?'

'When I'm good and ready. Jeez Ebony.' Brady laughed.

'Well you are a bit slow on the uptake.'

'Get used to us guys. We don't know what we're doing around women.'

'That's frigging obvious.'

They sat side by side at the table, handing photographs back and forth, revering the memory of Scarlett, sharing the story of each image.

'Dad, there's one thing I'd really like to do. I want to see the truck driver who hit Mum. And his wife Bren.' Ebony held her breath. 'They must have suffered a lot too.'

'Oh dear, yes, of course. Of course, they must.'

Forgiven

Brady rubbed the stubble on his chin absently. Making the decision to meet with Bren and John Burnside was one thing, but bringing it about was proving to be another thing altogether.

It should have been as easy as a phone call, a request, but it wasn't. Had he left things too long? What if it was too much for John? What if they didn't want to meet? After talking with Emma, Brady was aware of the emotional trauma John had suffered. And it can't have been much easier for his wife, Bren. Brady was ashamed he hadn't considered the effect on them. Lingering blame had been an oblique presence in his life, especially in the early days. He'd needed someone to blame. A scenario that made sense. A negligent driver, not a troubled wife— not a result of Scarlett's mental state.

For the first time he faced the very real possibility that Scarlett had used the accident to take her own life, surrender to her demons. That revelation shifted his anger to Scarlett, and brought fresh grief. How could she leave them that way? How could he ever forgive her? Or understand?

He might never know the truth, but the shared honesty with Ebony had proved a powerful bonding experience. He had to try and reach John Burnside somehow.

It was a new experience to face the past. However brief the conversation with Ebony, he knew they'd formed a tentative connection that was real. He hoped to build on that.

He felt more connected to his parents. He was thrilled to be able to work with his father to set up day-care for his mother. Jim had been as apprehensive as a new father on the first day of school, but Betty had taken to the weekly visits to the multi-purpose centre with enthusiasm. The staff had been welcoming and Betty was animated again.

Brady had commandeered Bill to take Jim fishing. He realised there were not only barriers in letting go of Betty's care, but his father had become isolated. It would take some time for him to adjust to socialising again.

But he was stymied when it came to meeting the Burnsides, and it was Jack who came up with a solution.

'Brady, why are you making a big deal out of this? There'll never be a right time,' said Jack.

'I'm probably over-thinking it,' said Brady.

'You reckon! You're acting like it's an international peace accord,' said Jack. 'Look, just have an ordinary night out with us, and Emma. She knows them well and John's been working on my office renovation. Have the kids there. An early tea at the Steakhouse would be good. There'll be other diners, so there won't be any pressure. Just let things happen; or not. Bren and John will be able to respond however they choose.'

A weathered surf lifesaving boat was suspended from the ceiling of The Steakhouse with taut wiring that also held triangular sails. This gave the restaurant an intimate feel without detracting from the high ceilings that were criss-crossed with timber beams.

On the tables, beer bottles had been transformed into salt and pepper shakers. Seemingly floating on air, a glossy cobalt drum kit was attached to a wall. Ancient number plates sat side by side with Pop Art Posters. The place was a blending of seaside and Rock & Roll. Rough-hewn timber benches and tables within walled off cubicles comprised the south end, and overlooking the ocean random timber tables and chrome chairs took precedence.

Jack and Helena, along with Jenna and Antonio were seated when Brady, Emma and Ebony arrived.

'Hello, party people.' Jenna greeted them with delight, dragging Antonio to an adjacent table, commandeering Ebony on her way.

Brady felt a moment of panic as he wondered how wise it was to include the others.

Jack slapped Brady on the back. 'This is good, Brady. Much time has passed. Let things happen.'

The girls began to fight over the kid's entertainment packs of colouring books and crayons, while Antonio looked on with amusement before joining in with gusto.

'How silly is that,' said Antonio, pointing to the wide screen television, 'showing surfing videos when we're already looking at the ocean.'

'Maybe that's the point, dufus,' said Jenna, jabbing him with her elbow.

Steve bounded in looking as if he'd just walked out of the surf and did a round of breezy hellos. He sat happily next to Ebony and was accused of reverting to Peter Pan by choosing the kid's table.

'We're not kids,' clamoured the girls.

Steve made a big deal of handing out the menus and teasing the girls by holding theirs just out of reach.

'Uncle Steve!' said Ebony, slapping his arm.

'What's this "uncle" business? You never call me that,' he said.

'Well, strictly speaking you're actually my *great* uncle.'

'Ouch! You really know how to hurt a guy.'

Ebony's stomach was a tense knot as she sat staring out at the twilight surf. Dad looked pale, and even Emma looked a little anxious. She caught her father's eye and gestured to the arched entrance of The Steakhouse. Bren and John had arrived.

Steve and Jack pulled the two tables together.

Brady approached John and Bren. 'I'm glad you came.' He smiled and shook both their hands.

John swallowed hard, started to speak and uttered a strangled sound. Bren tensed, and placed a reassuring hand on John's arm.

'Means a lot to us,' said John, taking the place at the table Jack offered.

Emma chatted with Bren as though they were continuing a familiar conversation they'd started earlier. Even though the meal went smoothly, John seemed to be having a tough time relaxing.

'Where's that fabulous Mexican sauce?' asked Helena, 'there's usually two on each table.'

'I'll get it,' said Brady, at the same time John rose from his chair. They walked together to the wait station where rows of the colourful bottles were lined next to serviettes and cutlery.

'Brady...Look, there's something I need to say.'

'Not for me. It's not necessary...'

'I need to say it *for me*, you know?' said John.

'Yeah. I get it.'

'I'm sorry. That's it.'

'And I'm sorry too, mate. I should've done this sooner. I've had my head in the sand.'

'Tell me about it!' said John.

'I've been so busy blaming, including myself. I didn't

let myself think about what it must have been like for you and Bren. It was easier to push you to the back of my mind as faceless, rather than a real person with life-changing consequences of your own.'

'It's getting better. And this, you can't know how much this means to Bren and me.'

'Same here, John. Same here.'

'Slow process, right.' said John.

'You're telling me.'

The two men grabbed sauce bottles and serviettes and returned to the meal. They sat apart from the others and talked while they ate. Later, Bren and Emma joined them.

The surfing video was replaced with music and the younger ones got up to dance. As they shook their energy out of their systems, the adults chatted over coffee. The music became slower and the teens returned to the table to order dessert. Brady invited Bren onto the dance floor, while Jack gathered Helena tenderly in his arms. Emma grabbed John and they were soon chatting.

After the music ended Brady joined the teens. 'Come on Eb, dance with your old man.'

'Ah, but you're so lame,' she said.

'Chicken.'

Ebony giggled and boogied her way over to her father. 'That was a great thing you did, Dad,' she said after a few minutes. 'I'd like to talk to him too, not to say much.'

'To let him know it's okay?' said Brady.

'Yeah. You can be real insightful sometimes, Dad.'

'So I'm not Dadzilla tonight.'

Ebony flushed. 'Nah, not tonight.'

When the song ended Ebony returned to Jenna and Antonio while Brady pulled Emma to him and kissed her soundly.

Sunday angst

'I told you your dad would come round, Eb. The dinner with Bren and John went really well.' Jenna flipped the kettle on.

'Yeah.'

'That's it? Just *yeah?*'

Ebony shuffled her feet. 'Well—I...'

The sound of the front door opening scattered Ebony's response. She threw a guilty look down the long hallway. Her father and Emma had returned from their wander along the beach. The morning promise of rain had become a soft timpani on the roof.

Jenna shrugged.

A plate clattered into the sink. Ebony and Jenna turned towards Bridget who was rinsing dishes.

Jenna moved towards Bridget. 'You okay Bridge?'

'Yeah. 'Course.'

'Your hands are trembling.'

'Whatever,' said Bridget. The word stabbed, jarring the two girls.

Bridget pulled a lank strand of hair behind her ear. She flushed. 'It's just...Jeez, I dunno. The things you two stress over.'

'Like what?'

'Your lives!' Bridget stared into the sink. 'I broke a plate.'

'Don't worry,' said Ebony, 'we'll do the dishes.'

'I gotta go anyway.' Bridget said.

The sounds of the television intruded. The Sunday musical tapped danced into the room, at odds with the tense mood.

Ebony's forehead creased. 'Bridget? Oh crap, you're bleeding.'

Bridget stared at her hand as crimson drops fell to the tiled floor, splattering carelessly. She seemed to be mesmerised by the sight. She slashed a hand across her damp forehead.

The storm outside exploded. The pale strobe of the television flashed and jarred down the hallway into the darkening room.

Turning slowly towards the girls, Bridget lifted her gaze. Then, her eyes rolled back as her body went limp.

Jenna lunged and broke her fall.

Ebony screamed, then called out. 'Dad! Emma!'

The house buzzed, shocked from Sunday bliss as Brady scooped Bridget up and carried her to the lounge room, where he lay her on the sofa.

'Throw me a tea towel, Eb—something to...thanks Jenna.' Emma balled the tea towel and held it on Bridget's hand.

'I'll...get a facecloth,' said Ebony, 'a wet one.' She was rewarded with a grateful look from Emma.

'Put her feet up Brady,' said Emma. She palpated the pulse at the base of the girl's pale wrist, now exposed as the gauzy sleeves of the shirt were free, revealing scars on Bridget's forearm. She flipped the cuffs down as she took the cool cloth from Ebony.

Ebony blanched at the sight, and stumbled back into Jenna.

Bridget's lashes fluttered. She moaned softly as Emma's words intruded. Then her eyes opened in alarm and she sat up, her breathing hard and fast.

'You fainted, Bridget,' said Emma, placing a hand on her shoulder, 'you might need to lie down for...'

Bridget put her hand over her mouth as harsh sobs fought to escape. 'No! Leave me! Alone!'

'Just let me dress the...'

Emma's hand was thrust aside as Bridget ran. Down the hall and out the front door.

'Bridget!' Jenna's voice was torn.

'What the hell?' Brady turned confused eyes on the girls.

'We have to go after her, Dad.' Ebony was already out the door, carrying a jade throw she'd grabbed off the lounge.

Brady and the girls checked the track through the bushland.

Emma drove the short distance to Bridget's home. There was no sign of the girl on the road. The car tyres spewed gravel on the driveway to the rundown Galloway house. The gloom of the place permeated the air. Emma rapped on the decaying screen door, and peered into the dark interior. A metallic clunk answered. Smoke from the wood heater that was lit on even the warmest day stifled the room.

Bridget's father appeared. He held a beer can and a cigarette in his left hand and gripped the large timber door with his right hand, opening it mere inches.

'I'm not buyin' nuthin',' he said, relishing a long drag on the cigarette, as he blew the smoke into Emma's face. He chuckled, and that liberty brought on a fit of coughing.

'I'm not a sales rep, Mr Galloway.' Emma paused, conscious of the reputation of the man in front of her. Bridget didn't deserve this. 'Is Bridget around?'

'Nah, she's prob'ly off with those stuck up friends of 'ers. Right little misses they are. Not that it's any of your bus'ness, Miss, what's yer name?'

'Emma Tesler.'

'Huh! That community nurse. Poking yer nose in are yer? Well, on yer bike darlin'. You got no truck pushing in ter our affairs. We don't need no welfare types.' The door closed a fraction. 'Ere, I tell yer wot—if yer do find 'er, tell 'er to get 'erself home ter cook me tea. Ta rah. Shove orf. Whatcha waitin' fer? Forms in triplicate? Ha Ha!'

The door slammed. Emma looked around. She'd heard of this place from her staff. The old man had broken his arm and been referred to the community nurses several years ago. He'd made short work of the girl who had come to see him.

The yard was littered with the usual accoutrements of a home that had once sustained life, but now contained only the detritus of that existence. An axe protruded awkwardly from a large block of wood, stuck there, probably left in a drunken stupor. Or maybe Tom Galloway was making some kind of point to the universe. He'd worked in the timber yard until he'd been sacked for operating machinery under the influence of alcohol. His wife had left a year later, although according to Galloway's version of events, it was her leaving that had unravelled his life.

Emma waited in the car for a few minutes. When there was no sign of Bridget, she returned to join Brady and the girls in the search.

They found Bridget an hour later, cold and trembling, curled into a hollowed tree trunk. The dead branches of the grey oak pointed impotently towards the dark sky, where thunder still threatened with dull Thor rumblings, and lightning shards flowered earthwards in the distance.

The storm was spent, and so was Bridget. Her eyes were wild, her body jerked. Ebony wrapped the throw around her.

Brady lifted Bridget into his arms. 'We must get her father.'

'No!' Ebony and Jenna shouted.

Brady looked to Emma. She shook her head. 'We'll take Bridget to A & E at the hospital. I'll phone ahead. She shouldn't be there long. A few blood tests. IV fluids will sort her out.

'Can we come?' Ebony's eyes were taut with anxiety.

'I guess,' said Brady, seeking Emma's approval.

'Sure,' said Emma, 'but you won't be able to go in with her. I'll take her in. You'll have to sit in the outpatients waiting area.' Emma stroked Bridget's face as Brady put her into the car. 'I want to get her home as soon as possible.'

'But, home is the problem,' said Jenna.

'I know you girls worry about Bridget. Her home life is problematic. It's hard for you to understand, but there is only so much that can be done. The best we can do right now is to get her sorted and home.'

'But,' sobbed Ebony.

'Bridget has to seek help,' said Emma.

Brady carried the limp girl into the A & E. A nurse

ushered them into the examination area. Emma scanned
the waiting room. Prudence Wainwright was watching
the scene intently. Emma moaned.

Questions rumble

Ecclesiastes, better known as Eccles, sniffed noisily through the garbage bin at Neville's feet. Eyeing her master through shaggy brows she gave a rumbling growl and crawled across the floor towards him. That trick usually won her master's attention but this time it failed. Neville was scribbling madly. Ecclesiastes rolled over and played dead.

Neville swore. He screwed another piece of paper into a ball and threw it in the bin with an exasperated moan. Tearing both hands through tangled hair he turned to the huge St Bernard.

'It's no use, Eccles.'

The dog leapt up at the sound of her name, tongue lolling. Eager to please her frustrated master she picked up the note Neville had discarded and brought it to him.

Neville laughed.

'I know, I should be marking papers, not writing poetry,' he said, looking at the mound of papers on his desk. 'But it *is* Sunday. I should have a day off, not be trying to motivate myself to mark assignments. You don't want to eat a little homework, do you? I've always wanted to use that line.'

Ecclesiastes rolled over to have her tummy rubbed.

'Now Eccles, why does that new girl in my class seem familiar? The one with hair like midnight. I guess you don't know, do you. How wonderful to be a dog and never have to ponder. You know why I have you, don't you, Eccles. Apart from the fact that I never have to mind my Ps and Qs. I have you so that no-one will ever know that I have a disturbing habit of talking to myself. And I can always rely on you to be in the same mood as me—not like our Scott.' Neville padded in socked feet to the kitchen where a large pot was simmering. 'Nearly ready Eccles. Yes, you love my spag bol. I wonder when Scott will want lunch. He's in the studio...and you know what that means. NO INTERRUPTIONS.'

Ecclesiastes made a gurgling growly sound.

'Ah yes, the only thing Scott hasn't painted is a DO NOT DISTURB sign. Perhaps we should paint one for him. No, you're right—he would *not* be amused. Well, if you're not going to eat the kids' homework, I'll have to get on with marking it. Or I could finish making lunch. Scott would like that. The smell might just bring him in from the man cave. You agree! Good choice, Eccles. I'll make lunch. Will you write me a note for school?'

Ecclesiastes raised expressive eyes that clearly

conveyed she would do anything in her power to make her master happy.

The buzz of his mobile phone on the table made Neville run before it flew off the table. He couldn't afford to break another one. This one was a gift from Scott.

'Hello, Neville Mangret speaking.'

'Oh, hello Mum, How are you … What are you doing at the hospital? … Slow down.'

'Your father had to have a tetanus shot.'

'At the hospital? Is he okay?'

'Of course he's okay. It's just a rusty fishing hook, that's all. He's been fishing with Jim Harcourt.'

'That's good Mum. Well, Dad must be pleased to have his fishing buddy back. Stop that Eccles. No, Mum, the dog just gets excited when we're on the phone. And she can smell lunch, I'm cooking spag bol.'

'Oh lovely, I won't keep you then. It's just that…' Estelle Mangret sighed. 'I guess it's confidential, but your father and I are worried and we don't know what to do.'

'What is it Mum?'

'Well…while we were going into the A & E we saw Jim's granddaughter and that girl she got into trouble with, you know, with the police—over that headmaster Brisley. Never did like him.'

'Mum!'

'Sorry, love. Well, we're not sure what was going on, but the staff were rushing around and we saw Dr James, he's the head psychiatrist. I wouldn't bother you but that busybody Prudence Wainwright was there with her batty friend and they were whispering about some kid attempting suicide. I told them off. God only knows what they knew and what they were making up as they went along. It's just that Bill worries about Jim. We both do. He's been through so much in the past few years, what with Betty and all. And there was that dreadful accident with the daughter-in-law. Oh, must be over three years ago now.'

'Mum, you're losing me. I don't know why you're telling me all this, love. I don't know how I can help, other than listen. What's this about? Or who? Dad or someone else?'

'Listen Neville, it's about Jim's granddaughter, Ebony Harcourt. Poor little pet, mind she's a teenager now. She's a student at the school. I thought you might know her. You are the welfare teacher.'

'I do. She started this year. She's a good kid, smart and conscientious. What's this about her mother in an accident?'

'She was killed on the highway. Not that far from your place, if I remember rightly. I thought you'd know all about it. John Burnside was coming home from Melbourne in the truck. The woman came out of nowhere. Killed instantly, they said. Wandering in her nightgown. You must remember her. Bit of an artist, she was in one of Scott's holiday classes if I recall. Jim's son Brady never got over it. There was talk it was suicide. Jim said they didn't get any answers.'

'I heard about John Burnside killing a woman while driving his truck. They lost the business, haven't been the same since.'

'The woman was Jim's daughter in law—had some mental illness or another. Anyway, Prue Wainwright was saying that history must have repeated itself. The daughter attempting suicide.'

'Oh my God.'

'Look, son. It might be a rumour, but I wanted to tell you about the girl. Apparently she's the spitting image of the mother, I think her name was Violet or Scarlett, some bright colour. Neville, are you still there?'

'Yes, Mum. I'm here.'

'You remember?'

'I remember.'

After he hung up, Neville went to the spare room. Flicking a calico cover aside on a huge canvas, he looked for a long time at the image of the back of a glorious dark-haired woman in a crimson dress. He'd wondered why Scott kept the painting in the spare room.

Anxiety clenched his stomach. The noonday sun blazed down on the long narrow yard as Neville stared at Scott's studio, just visible behind the dense group of May bushes at the edge of their five acre property.

'I need to talk to Scott about this, Eccles.' Dragging himself from the window, Neville went into the kitchen. Once the sauce was simmering on the stove top and the pasta had been thrown into the pot, he sat at the dining table and stared out of the window.

'He's not going to want to talk about it,' he said, no longer sure if he was talking to the dog that lay at his feet, or a ghost from the past. There was so much about that night he didn't understand.

Scott had been packing for an overseas exhibition, with only a few hours before the airport cab was due to take him to Sydney Airport. Like tonight, Neville had been marking year end essays when he heard loud voices. A distraught woman's voice rose then dipped into a sob. 'I want it back. It's important.'

'Scarlett. It's already in New York, you know that.'

'I don't want it sold. Get it back.'

Neville had glanced at his watch. 2 am. It was unusual for students to visit in the early hours of the morning, unless it was an after-class party for the art group. He hadn't seen the woman arrive. Scott's deep voice had rumbled. 'It might already be sold, Scarlett. Most of them have been viewed online. You know some of the works are set aside and pre-paid if there's an interest.'

'God no! But the exhibition hasn't started. I don't want

it sold, to anyone. Not *to anyone!*' The woman cried pitifully.

Neville strained to hear the words. He made it a practice to never get involved with Scott's work, but there was something about the angst in the woman's voice brought him into the hallway.

The woman had turned, her eyes were wild and damp. She stumbled hard against the wall, something like fear in her eyes. Scott had tried to soothe her, but his voice only increased her agitation. Spreadeagled against the wall, the woman stared at Neville. For several tense moments, the only sound that filled the house was her rapid breathing. An icy draught slammed the heavy front door up against the wall behind Neville.

The sound echoed through the house. Neville instinctively reached out a hand to the woman as she twisted a ring on her finger. It was then Neville realised she wasn't looking at him, but her gaze was fixed on the darkness outside.

In a ragged flash she was gone, running for her life into the night.

Scott had buckled in a weary heap. He sat on the edge of the bed in the spare room as Neville approached.

'What on earth was that about, Scott? Who was that?'

'Scarlett Harcourt. One of my students—a brilliant one. She has a self-portrait in the group exhibition, but she's changed her mind. She seemed thrilled about selling it. I don't understand. Don't slobber on that, Eccles. Neville, take that damn dog away.'

Neville delivered a quick tap to the dog's nose. 'What can you do?'

Scott leaned down to help. 'I had to promise not to show it. I gave her that ruby antique ring she'd admired as payment if the painting had already sold, but that only made her more upset. The painting is stunning. It could've really put her on the map.'

'The woman in the red dress?'

Scott nodded.

'You told me about her. I thought she was really excited. What was it you said—"beyond cloud nine"?'

'Too far above cloud nine, I'm afraid. She's bipolar.' Scott dragged trembling fingers through his hair.

'Oh,' said Neville. 'Did you meet her in group therapy?'

'No, she turned up out of the blue, said she'd been an art student at Sydney Uni. She doesn't know I've twigged to the bipolar. I only know because I found a foil medication packet in the rubbish. She's supposed to be on the same medication as I was.'

'You're sure? About the diagnosis?'

'She's too much like me to leave doubt. She's been manic the past two weeks.'

'Complicated. I wonder why she changed her mind.' Neville patted Eccles and took a biscuit out of his pocket, delivering it to the grateful pooch.

'I wish you wouldn't do that Neville. It's unhygienic. I suppose you wander around teaching the kids with pockets full of dog biscuits.'

'Only when I forget to empty them.'

Scott moaned. 'You're such a style wasteland Nev. Hell, look at the time. Help me get my cases to the front door.'

In a matter of minutes the cases had been rolled noisily over the timber flooring. Both men stood in the front room. Neville adjusted Scott's scarf.

'Oh, *now* you're a style icon,' muttered Scott, tucking the scarf into his cashmere coat.

'Can you get the painting back?' Neville cracked his knuckles causing Scott to wince.

'Do you have to do that, you know I hate it,' said Scott. 'She has my number. If she still wants it back, I'll have to send it, I suppose. I'll wait to hear from her. She's just as likely to change her mind again.'

'Will she be alright?

'God only knows.'

'You were very calm.' Neville's mouth curved in a grim smile.

'Remind me never to yell at you again, ever. I'd forgotten how horrendous it is to be on the receiving end.'

A car horn blasted. The airport cab had ended the conversation.

Neville slumped into the nearest kitchen chair, his hand limply resting on Eccles, who took the opportunity to wash her master's fingers with her dripping tongue. Neville didn't appear to notice this generosity.

This was the first time Neville had made the connection with their night visitor and the tragic accident on the highway. Scott had returned from the exhibition with an episode of low grade depression. He'd brought the painting back, and it had been stored in their spare room since, forgotten.

Now, he knew why Ebony was so familiar. She certainly resembled her mother. The teacher's staffroom had been rife with gossip after Brisley had been caught in flagrante with the librarian by the two girls. While no one was sure why the girls had been at the librarian's house at the time, it was rumoured the girls were on a mission. They'd had their heads stuck together in the library on the computers going through old newspaper articles.

'Newspapers, that's it, Eccles.' Neville brought his laptop to the table, he could do with the comfort of the sunlit room. When he found what he wanted, he opened the desktop folder with the recent school photos. It was time to call Scott. He'd be ready for lunch anyway.

'Scott, we need to talk. Yes, now, it's lunchtime anyway. Mum phoned. One of my students...oh, just come!'

In only minutes Scott appeared at the back door. After

a brief scrubbing in the utility room sink, he grabbed a bread roll from the kitchen. 'Is that spag bol I smell? Great, I'm starving.'

'Forget food, forget yourself for once.'

'Okay, but you know I can't think on an empty stomach.'

Neville snorted and quickly slapped food onto a plate and handed it to Scott.

'You going to eat? Gosh Nev, what has got you in a twist? One of your kids in trouble?'

'Sort of, well, I think we, I mean you, might have answers.'

'Me? Answers? Answers for who?'

'*Whom*. What does it matter? Maybe us, maybe the girl, I don't know...'

'You are in a state, love. Don't get your knickers in a knot.'

Neville sat down, head in hands. Ecclesiastes licked his elbow. 'Even the dog has more heart than you.'

'If you think that's the way to get me on board you can think again.' Scott sighed. 'I do wish you'd start making sense, love.'

Neville flipped the laptop open.

Scott peered at the screen. 'I haven't got my glasses. You know I can't read a thing without them.'

Neville produced Scott's glasses and pointed. 'That photograph Scott.'

'Is that the kid you're talking about? Wait on, she's familiar. That's, that's the woman who was here that night. I never heard back about her painting. I still have it. It's...'

'In our spare room, I know. So you remember the face?'

'Of course I do. Scarlett Harcourt was a woman you could never forget. The luminosity of her talent, the atmospheric quality of her art. It was sublime. I always wondered why she didn't phone me about the painting. She must've been happy to accept the ring as payment, I suppose. What's she doing in the paper? An art exhibition?'

'This isn't Scarlett, Scott. It's her daughter, Ebony. Scarlett died that night. We may have been the last people to see her alive.'

Scott's face drained of colour.

'Oh my God, I thought that girl was Scarlett. She looks so much like her mother. What do you mean? Scarlett dead? Not that night!'

Neville turned the laptop around and leaned over it. 'Here, I'll read the article to you'.

He cleared his throat and began—'"A motor vehicle accident claimed the life of a pedestrian in the early hours of the morning of the 16th. A 34 year old woman, clad only in a nightie, was struck by a truck on the M1 highway. The truck driver, John Burnside, a local transportation company owner, was on his way home from an interstate delivery. He was treated at the scene for shock. There will be an inquest into the death, but police sources report that there are no suspicious circumstances. Mr Burnside returned a negative reading for drugs and alcohol. No charges have been laid. The deceased, Mrs Scarlett Harcourt, was holidaying with family. She is survived by her husband and twelve year old daughter".'

'The sixteenth—the day I left. God Nev, she was walking. I thought she'd come by car. I let her walk.'

Neville paused, then sat at the table. 'Mum said there was a question of suicide, but the inquest was inconclusive.'

'Oh Neville, not suicide surely. And now the daughter, is that a possibility? History repeating.'

Neville shook his head. 'God, I hope not.'

'Poor Scarlett. And I let her walk out in that terrible state of mind. What did the paper say? She was in her nightie of all things. Odd that—she was wearing a gorgeous red coat when she was here, designer wool, Veronika Maine, if I remember. God have mercy. Walking alone and distraught.'

'I'm afraid to ask, but ... did anything happen before that night?'

'I don't know love, I'm struggling to remember. I know she'd gone off her meds so she could paint again, didn't want to be dulled down. Well, there was a woman, a student in the class, Carla something. They had a few tense words. Scarlett was pretty upset. Oh God, Nev, she walked onto the road in the truck's path. Wearing nothing but a bloody nightie.'

'And that fancy ring,' Neville added.

'The antique, with the ruby, she loved that thing, she was always teasing me about it—saying they were a match made in heaven. Wanted me to sell it to her, but I wouldn't. She swanned around with it on in class the day I had them sketch jewellery. Dead. I can't believe it. She was so playful, so full of life. I wondered why she didn't contact me. It's unbearable. What must the family have gone through? That kid.'

'That kid needs answers, Scott.'

'And so do we, my love, so do we.'

'Any ideas?

'Well, I'd sure like to follow her footsteps for that night as best we can. Where would she have walked?

Neville turned the laptop towards him. 'I'll google our house. That'll be a start. Where was Scarlett staying at the time? Do you know, Scott?'

'She was staying with the in-laws.'

'That would be the Harcourts. Betty and Jim. My dad knows Jim, they go fishing together.'

'Yes, that would be right. I remember Scarlett talking about them. She was really fond of the old couple. Where the heck do they live?'

Neville checked the directory. 'They live on Fisher's Cove Road. Number 4. Write that down Scott. The son must live next door with his daughter, Ebony. He had some fancy corporate job in Sydney, but moved back to Noarlunga.'

Scott stretched his legs. Neville typed in the details, and they both stared at the screen as the route appeared on the screen.

'Shit,' said Scott. 'It's a long way by road. She must've cut through the scrub. She would've gone through Old Galloways' property.'

A chill crept into the room as they silently contemplated the tragedy, and what they were undertaking.

That ruby purse

'I told yer to shove orf yesterday, Missie.' Tom Galloway shuffled to the door. 'Interferin' busy body.' He stumbled on a footstool in the cramped lounge room and cursed all furniture and most people. Where was Bridget? She usually answered the door. He had half a mind to stay put, but he'd called out, so there was nothing for it except to answer the sharp rapping and send the caller on their way.

'Who are you?' he said.

'Neville Mangret, Mr Galloway. I'm a teacher at the school. I teach your daughter, Bridget. Um...' Scott elbowed him. 'Ouch, Scott!'

'Spit it out mate. Then get lost. I told that bloody nurse to keep 'er nose out of m'business and the same applies ter you. I don't need no help with my family. My daughter aint home.'

'Listen Galloway, we're not here to bother anyone,' said Scott. 'We live in the house that backs on to your property. This is just a courtesy call. We wanted your permission to...What Neville?'

'We just want to walk across your land, the bush at the

side Mr Galloway. That's all,' said Neville.

'What?' Galloway's face flushed red. His fists clenched at his side. 'How dare yers! Y'bloody...Get goin' now! Don't come near me land, not now, not ever. I'll have yer fer trespassin'. Yer hear me??'

Scott stepped back and the ancient timber steps gave way. Neville reached for him, whipping his arm around Scott's back.

The door slammed.

'Sheesh, what's his beef?' said Scott, 'it's just a bit of scrub, not the Taj Mahal.'

'Goodness knows. Let's get out of here.'

The front door opened behind them and a beer bottle flew through the air, landing in the middle of the driveway just behind them as they walked.

'Just as well I left the car on the footpath.' Scott brought the keys out of his pocket. 'Oh crap, will you look at that? How did that happen? That's all we need—a flat tyre.'

'I'll help you. This place gives me the spooks.'

Scott bent down to inspect the tyre. 'There are builder's tacks here. The old bugger probably puts them here deliberately.'

'Thank goodness there's a huge hedge here. Who knows what other missiles the old bugger will throw.'

Scott wrestled the spare out of the boot, and Neville looked over his shoulder.

'I thought you were going to help me Neville. Stop

chewing your nails. The old bloke's too drunk to do any real harm.'

'If his reputation is anything to go by that's when he does the most harm,' muttered Neville.

While Scott changed the tyre Neville filled him in on the local gossip about Tom Galloway. Neither of them saw his son, Byron Galloway, creeping towards the hedge and position himself behind a derelict car carcass. With the amount of marijuana in his room, Byron wanted to know what the two men were about, especially if they intended to wander around his domain.

'I think we should still go, through the bush I mean. It will help to trace Scarlett's footsteps that night,' Neville said, idly rocking the tyre iron from hand to hand while Scott positioned the jack.

'Yes, but I want to be sure old Galloway isn't watching, or following. I don't want him interfering,' said Scott. 'I'm even more curious now. It was bloody cold that night. I really want to know what happened. She was dressed to the nines when she left us, carrying that ruby purse.'

'A purse? I don't remember a purse.'

'Well, she had it that night. I remember her struggling to pull it out of her coat pocket to get the money.'

'The article didn't say anything about those.' Scott tightened the last nut on the tyre with expert fingers. 'But it didn't mention the coat. That has me puzzled.'

'They said there were no suspicious circumstances, so

I guess they didn't bother. I'm not sure what we hope to gain, but I'd rather have as many cards in the deck as I can before I push myself into someone's life and wreak havoc. If they never found the purse or the coat that would be really odd. Maybe someone intervened. But then again, they might have found them—they don't put everything in the papers.'

'The cops did search the area. I remember that from talk around the place,' said Neville. 'What are we going to do about that other woman? The one in your art class?'

'Carla? Yes. She might be able to shed some light. I got the feeling they knew each other from somewhere else.'

'Maybe we could see her first. Give Galloway time to get legless. Do you know where she lives?'

'Yeah, she looks after that café and gallery at McLaren Vale, in the vineyards.'

'The place with the hand-painted jackets you love, Scott?'

'Thanks for reminding me. I might buy one while we're there. If you promise not to ruin it, you fashion retard. Here, get me a rag from the boot.' Scott rummaged through his pockets.

'Honestly, I don't know what you'd do without me. What are you looking for?'

'My mobile. I'll google Carla's number and send her a text.'

Byron didn't hear the last sentence. His thoughts had become a whirlpool. Hell, he'd forgotten about that night. The night he'd been out roaming and off his face. He was only fifteen at the time, but the memory was burned into his brain. Like train carriages shunting brutally into each other memories of that night slammed together. A night he'd rather forget and until that moment he thought he'd done a pretty good job. Forgetting he'd picked up a red shiny purse some wailing woman had dropped in the bush as she bolted past his secret smoking place. A stupid fancy purse that had no cash in it, just a few scribbled notes that looked like lists. He'd kept it anyway, stuffed at the back of his wardrobe, behind his bag of hash. It had looked expensive—he'd thought he might get something for it one day. Hell, he was just a kid.

The cops had been everywhere for a day or two, asking questions. They would have found the damn purse if he'd thrown it somewhere, cops were good at that sort of thing. He'd wished he'd left it alone, but it was too late then. He'd mumbled some sort of answers and they'd left him alone.

No-one knew he'd been anywhere near the bush that night, having a quiet smoke. He'd hidden every sign he'd ever been there, and he'd never been back. The cops hadn't made much effort for long. The woman's death was deemed accidental. There'd been no mention of a purse in the papers.

After the court case, he'd forgotten about the purse,

and the cops. His father might be a useless drunk, but he wasn't on the police radar. Well, not since his mother had left and the few neighbours that cared had stopped ringing the cops when his old man was beating his mother.

But with these two guys poking around, that might change. The cops might reopen an investigation and come sniffing around the house. He shuddered. He didn't need that. He had quite a stash of grass. He felt like a spliff just thinking about it.

Paranoia set in as he considered the pros and cons.

It would be better if these two blokes found the purse. Then he'd be off the hook. He hadn't taken anything out of it. He'd been disappointed that such a fancy looking thing had contained nothing of value.

Byron waited until the car disappeared down the road, then with quick steps, he covered the ground between the bush and the house. He took the purse from his wardrobe, wiped it over with bleach and strode to the fence.

Once there, he bent down and scuffed the purse in the dirt and leaves, then arced it into the air towards the scrub, in the direction of the winding dirt track on the other side from his secret place. Away from the smell of his hash.

Carla remembers

Carla was dealing with a customer when her phone beeped. As she rang the purchase up, she saw the message was from Scott Dan, her art tutor. She hadn't seen him for years. A thread of apprehension wove around her nerves.

'Oh, I don't know.' The customer blustered. 'Maybe I should...'

Carla's hands stilled on the phone. Scott Dan, what did he want? His name teased a part of her past she'd tried to forget.

'What do you think, dear?' asked the woman

Carla forced herself to concentrate on the customer in front of her. The woman had been there for an hour trying to decide on a painting for her husband. 'Do you want to look around a bit more?

The woman stiffened. 'Never mind dear. I've taken enough of your time.'

'No, No. I'm sorry, Madam. I'm sure your husband would love either painting.'

The woman smiled and put both paintings on the

counter. Carla took extra care gift wrapping them. She kept up a nervous patter of conversation. She couldn't afford to offend customers.

When the woman finally left Carla retrieved Scott's message. It was short, but it rocked her.

> Hi Carla, Scott Dan here. Can we catch up, darls? Need some info on Scarlett Harcourt – was Camberwell. Free this arvo? Ciao.

Scarlett and Carla curled into the velvet couch that overlooked her parent's garden. A fine mist of rain softened the view and wept onto the windows in slow streams that zigged and zagged. Bridal magazines and menus lay strewn across the Persian rug. Used coffee cups covered a glass low table, their darkened residue testament to a long morning's work.

'This wedding gig is hard work Scarlett,' said Carla, smoothing her auburn curls as she slapped a magazine shut and threw it to slide across the others.

Scarlett draped a tired arm over the side of the chair. 'Yes,' she sighed. 'But there's so little time left. Brady graduates this weekend and the wedding is two weeks after that.'

Carla brushed cake crumbs from her skirt. 'Are you sure about this, Scarlett?' She cast worried eyes over her friend. 'It's just so quick, you've only known him a few months.'

Scarlett wrenched herself upright. 'Look, I know what I'm doing. I'm sorry if you feel let down. I know we'd planned to share a house. But don't you see? Everything has changed. I have Brady...'

Carla sighed, her eyes pained. 'Scarlett, it's not about house-sharing. I'm worried about you. I care about you. We've been friends since middle school, been through a lot together. I'd hate you to go through what you did again.'

'How dare you bring that up! That was years ago. I was just a kid.' Scarlett clenched both hands at her side.

'I know. I was there remember. It was really hard to see you like that. It wasn't just tough for you, you know.'

Scarlett stood and paced the room with angry steps. 'Don't ruin this for me, Carla. If you even think of telling...*anyone, ever.*'

'You mean you haven't told Brady?' Carla stilled. 'It's...something you need to share with him. If he found out another way...someone is bound to say something one day. Things like that have a habit of coming out. It would be better coming from you. Then you'd have nothing to worry about. Brady is a great guy. He'd understand, he would.'

'No! You don't understand, Brady is my *everything*.' Scarlett's voice was cold. 'This is my decision. I can't believe you'd threaten to tell him.'

'Oh Scarlett. I wasn't threatening to tell him. You know me better than that. I would never tell him. Or anyone else. I just assumed you'd told him.' Carla stretched out a hand to touch Scarlett's shoulder.

Scarlett jerked away. 'It was just...depression. Everyone goes through that. I don't know what else you think you know, but that's all it was.'

'But you were in hospital. You can't keep that a secret.'

'Why not. It's confidential. No one at school knew.'

'Of course they did, they talked.'

'Rumours,' said Scarlett, reinventing history. 'Just rumours.' She lifted a defiant chin and glared at Carla.

Carla paled at the slice of panic in Scarlett's eyes. 'Look, I'm on your side, Scarlett. Please don't get me wrong.'

Scarlett sliced a thin arm through the tense air. 'I think...I think it's best if you don't come to the wedding. I can't trust you...not anymore.' Scarlett folded her arms, turned her back and stared at the garden. 'You can leave now.'

Raising her hands in surrender, Carla picked up her handbag. As she opened the door to leave Elise Camberwell swished in with Tony in tow, hardly visible behind a pile of boxes.

'Hello, Carla, nice to see you,' laughed Elise. 'Don't trip over Tony, he's an unwilling work horse today.'

'What do you mean today?' said Tony. 'Hi Carla. Staying for lunch? I could do with some sane company.'

Scarlett cut in. 'Carla is just leaving.'

'Goodbye, Mrs Cam...Elise, Tony.'

'What's that about?' asked Elise. 'Scarlett?'

Scarlett smiled brightly. 'Nothing, Mother. Nothing at all.'

Carla cringed at the cold words. She turned as the door closed behind her then ran to the solace of the dense shrubbery where her shivering tears found release.

Strangers

The afternoon sun blazed through the window of Jim and Betty Harcourt's kitchen. A breeze gently tugged the white gauze curtains as the sun's rays lifted and dipped across the cork floor, casting a combination of soft shadows and amber glow.

'School finish early?' Jim Harcourt stomped through the back door and eyed Ebony and Jenna with suspicion. The girls straightened in the kitchen chairs. The aroma of coffee lingered in the air hinting they'd been there a while.

Ebony hiccupped.

'Oh *really*, Ebony?' Jenna gave Jim her most charming smile.

Jim Harcourt frowned. 'Don't worry girls, I'm not going to phone the truancy officer.'

'But Grandie, there was an excursion and we...Ouch, Jenna, what was that for?'

Jim frowned. 'I think that kick was to let you know to quit while you're ahead, Ebony. You're an appalling liar, a trait I greatly admire, so stitch it up will you.'

Betty wandered into the room, spilling biscuit crumbs from the Assorted Creams packet that was half open.

'Oh Betty!' Jim rushed to take the packet. 'Time for your nap.'

'She's alright, Grandie.' Ebony found herself on the receiving end of a rare but stern look from her grandfather. 'Sorry, night, Nan.'

As Jim led Betty from the room he patted her tangled hair. He paused at the door. His eyes were wistful. 'Don't go anywhere, Eb. I'll be back in a jiffy.'

'I'd better be going, Eb,' said Jenna. 'I think your Grandie wants to have a talk with you. Best I take off.'

Ebony nodded and mutely escorted Jenna to the front door of her grandparents' unit.

'Who's that at your place?' asked Jenna, pointing to a sleek yellow sports car.

'Dunno,' said Ebony, 'wasn't there when we arrived.'

'Might have been. We came in the back way, remember?' Jenna hugged Ebony, slipped her backpack over one shoulder and made a sign to Ebony with her hand "phone me".

Ebony mouthed "okay" and turned to go inside. She bumped into her grandfather's bulk.

'Oh, Grandie. I love you.' she leaned into his familiar comfort. She inhaled the earthy smell of his checked flannelette shirt.

Jim wrapped his arms around her.

'We have visitors. Who are they, Grandie?'

'Best you go and see, pet. I'm not sure anyway, but I think you might be going to get some of those answers you've been looking for.'

Brady leapt from his seat and brought his daughter into the lounge room, his arm firmly around her shoulders.

Ebony's eyes struggled to adjust to the interior of the house. 'Hi Dad,' she said, almost shyly.

There were three other people in the room. She was confused but heartened to see that one of them was her history teacher, Neville Mangret. He smiled. Another man sat beside him. A woman on the third lounge was a stranger. She was curvy and had short flame-coloured hair. There was a sense of composed calm about her. All three visitors leaned into the room, focused on her. They seemed uncertain whether to stand.

Brady began the introductions. 'Eb, you know Mr Mangret, ah, I should start with the lady. This is Carla, she was a student when your mother and I were at Uni. She was a friend of your mother's, and mine. And this is Scott Dan, he's Neville's partner and an artist.' Brady cleared his throat. 'Of some renown I'm told.' He gave his daughter a weak smile. 'And that's about all I know because I told them I wanted to wait for you.'

Ebony sat bunched up next to her father.

'Yes, we didn't want, er, to go ahead until you got here.

Oh dear, Scott you start.' Neville Mangret leaned back into the lounge with a sigh.

'He's a big softie,' said Scott.

'I know,' said Ebony. 'He's my favourite teacher.'

'Really,' said Neville, 'oh that's so sweet. I thought all the kids...'

'Put a damper on it Nev.' Scott rolled his eyes.

'Well, excuse me, Mr Famous Artist, I don't get much praise, pardon me if I enjoy a little...'

'They're like this all the time,' said the woman, Carla. 'Come on Ebony, let's get some coffee. Show me the way to the kitchen.'

Ebony jumped to her feet, glad of the reprieve. In minutes the coffee was percolating. 'I've never met any of my mother's friends. There's so much I'd like to know. Her life seems like a closed door or something.'

'I think that's the way she wanted it, Ebony. Do you want to sit for a bit? We can steal a quick catch up while the boys argue. Will your dad survive?'

'He'll have to,' said Ebony. She was warming to this direct woman. 'You're not like my mother. Well I don't know, I guess...'

Carla smoothed her long jade skirt. 'Oil and water, that was us. We'd known each other since primary school you know. I think I was terribly bossy with her at times. She was such a free spirit. So impulsive, so...'

'Wild?'

'A little. She took risks. But that's what made her a good artist. While I was painfully sketching dandelions, your mother was splashing colour over canvases like there was no tomorrow. That's how she approached everything, as if life was a dream she'd wake from. As if everything was transient and she was just, I don't know, an ethereal spirit child.'

'I guess I never saw that.'

'I think that's why she fell so hard for your father. He brought such stability.'

'She loved him then?'

'Quite desperately.'

'Oh, I guess it's hard to think of your parents that way.'

'She had to work hard to get him mind you. Oh speak of the devil, hello Brady, come to check up on the working class?'

'Carla, you never change.' Brady smiled. 'I've missed you, you know. Carla lives around here, Ebony.'

'Oh, really, that's great.'

'Yes sweetie, you and I are going to be great friends. We have so much to talk about.' Carla laughed.

'Not about me I hope,' said Brady.'

'Plenty about you Brady. Did you know your father introduced himself as Mr Boring Pratt, Ebony?'

'Really?' Ebony looked quizzically at her father.

'Dastardly rumour, Eb. Don't believe a work this woman says. Come on girls, the natives are getting restless. Mr Mangret, Neville, wants a hot chocolate because a coffee will put his nerves over the edge and Scott is going to beg for whiskey in his if we take much longer.' Brady grabbed mugs. 'Are you okay Eb?'

'I think I'm going to be, Dad. Better than that—I think we are going to be fine.'

Tears formed in Brady's eyes. 'You make an old guy proud, Eb. I love you.'

'I love you too, Dad. To the Milky Way and back.'

'You're not just talking about a chocolate Milky Way are you, because I'd really like to rate higher than a chocolate.'

Ebony linked her arm through his. This made the tray in Brady's hands wobble perilously, but he didn't care. They sat together on the lounge, neither picked up their mugs. A sigh shuddered from Ebony. She raised fearful eyes to her father.

Carla looked at the men sipping their coffee and sighed. 'Let's stop beating around the bush fellas.'

'Thanks Carla. We don't know where to start,' said Scott.

'How much do you know about your mother's health, Ebony?'

'She seemed, I don't know, like all the edges had been dulled or...it's hard to explain. She was vulnerable, I saw that.' Ebony's eyes misted. She wiped her eyes quickly, grateful that Carla hadn't been discomforted or tried to say the right thing, like most of the adults in her life.

'There was that always that underlying frailty. You knew she had bipolar?'

'Yes. Dad told me.' Ebony's eyes widened. She hadn't expected the conversation to be this honest.

'I'm glad he told you. Lots of people don't. They treat it like some shameful secret.' Carla took a sip from her coffee then put it down. 'In truth, that was one of Scarlett's problems.'

The room was quiet except for the dull roar of the surf. A radio played in the distance and a lawnmower started up, far enough away to avoid shredding the stillness.

'Keeping her mental illness a secret was a great disservice to Scarlett. I think it made her feel shame and no one needs that. I don't know if we'll get very many answers today. Sometimes in life, we just have to live with the questions.' Carla looked at Ebony. 'Can you deal with that, Ebony?'

'I only want to know as much of the truth as there is to know. I don't want to feel like, like Mum was a stranger with some sort of dark unspoken past. It makes her seem so out of reach, so unknowable. I was twelve when she died. I have memories. I want them to mean something. Have somewhere to belong.'

Neville pulled out a handkerchief and wiped his eyes. Scott patted his knee.

'Scarlett attempted suicide when we were in high school.'

Ebony felt her father stiffen. 'I didn't know that,' he said.

'You were never supposed to know. Scarlett's parents took her home from the hospital. They hired a private nurse and told everyone she had a virus. They were desperate to keep it a secret. All her friends were turned away. I don't think I was the only one who knew the truth. Scarlett talked about it at first, to me. And then she just clammed up. Pretended it never happened. I wanted her to tell your father. We fought over it actually.'

'Before the wedding,' said Brady, 'that's what the row in the kitchen was about—the reason you weren't a bridesmaid.'

'Yes. I stayed away after that. I heard a bit through the grapevine, just that you and Scarlett had a baby girl, and that Scarlett had been diagnosed with bipolar. I read up on it then, things started to fit together. I moved away the next year. It was a shock to see Scarlett in Scott's classes. I was so glad to see her. I still have some of her paintings you know. Early ones of course. I thought she'd be pleased to see me, I'd missed her, missed us, our friendship. We used to do everything together as teens. But she was so afraid of anyone finding out about the suicide attempt. At least that what I assumed, but she didn't make much sense that day. She kept saying "It wasn't you, Carla, it was never about you. It was him, it was always him".'

'Do you know who she meant?' asked Brady.

'I didn't have a clue what she was talking about. She could be quite irrational at times. I'd tried to invite her to our place. She used to hang out with my husband, Jeff and I at school. She and I babysat Jeff's younger sister. Jeff's parents were in town and I thought she'd have moved past all the former stuff, and want to come for a visit. But she was frantic, she was upset about some painting. She kept saying "Everyone wants to buy it, *everyone*". I was so hurt and confused. Oh I'm sorry, I've turned into a watering pot.'

Brady rose and found a box of tissues. 'Should have thought of this earlier,' he said, handing it to Carla.

'I'll have some of those,' said Scott, grabbing for a handful of tissues. 'I thought you must have known her before, Carla.'

'God, will you look at me, snivelling like a baby. I didn't know Scarlett had died until a few days ago. We've been running around like mad things, but I'd better follow the lovely Carla's example and start at the beginning...'

Between

No one noticed the low orb of the sun simmer down the evening ladder of the night sky, through orange-crimson shades until it settled just on the horizon, winked at the world and slipped to the other side of the earth.

Neville had joined Scott in the storytelling in a "to and fro" that was part argument and part narrative as they added and interjected in that way people in tune with each other have conversed for centuries.

'It was pelting down'

'bucketing'

'he was muddy, what a sight'

'covered in leaves and muck'

'totally.'

'we lost the umbrella'

'lost all track of time'

'he wouldn't give up'

Neville dragged a sports bag in front of him

'...Then we found it,' said Scott, proudly pulling the ruby purse out of the bag and handing it to Brady. 'Could someone turn a light on. Where has the time gone?'

'Oh my,' said Brady, touching it reverently, 'Scarlett's purse. I wondered where that was. Where ever did you find it?'

Ebony reached out and turned a light on.

'On the fence line. She must have been nearly home when she dropped it. I don't know.' said Scott.

'She must have gone back, been disoriented in the night. It was dark and cold. But it's strange that it should be found now. I thought the police searched the area.' Brady stared at the purse. 'It doesn't look as if it's seen much weathering, it's quite...clean. How odd.'

'You said the police decided quite early that there were no suspicious circumstances. I guess they didn't think it was necessary to search too thoroughly.' Neville shrugged.

'Some questions never have answers, Brady,' said Carla.

'We'll never know, Dad. It's all right, really, it's all right.' Ebony's fingers itched to hold the purse, but she could wait. 'Wow, it must have been gorgeous once, what a lovely colour.'

'There are some tears,' said Carla. 'I have a wonderful woman who sews for the gallery. I can get her to fix it if you like Ebony.'

'That would be wonderful, Carla.' Ebony handed Carla the purse. 'I'd love to see the gallery too.'

Brady couldn't stop staring at the purse. 'I can't believe it was there after all this time. I'm thrilled you guys found it. And thanks Scott, thanks for telling us. I'm so glad you're the one who gave her the ring.'

'That's fine, Brady. I hope you didn't lose sleep ... oh dear, you did. I know that look. Well, now you know.'

'I can't thank any of you enough. I'm sorry it's so late. Please let me feed you. Pizza anyone?'

'Thought you'd never ask,' said Neville.

'Where are your manners, Nev,' said Scott. 'You're such a Hoover when it comes to food. Never puts an ounce on. It's depressing. Alright, I'll have Hawaiian. Carla?'

'I'd better get home to Jeff and the kids,' she said. 'But...' she sat forward expectantly.

Scott and Neville were strangely quiet. It took Brady a moment to realise that everyone was staring at the purse. He felt a chill. He didn't want to think about what was inside. Four years of apprehension and doubt niggled.

Brady drew in a deep breath and opened the catch. 'No rust, that's a wonder,' he said. 'Some paper, looks like a list of art supplies and a note of some sort. Look at that later. Key...hmm.'

'That looks like the one I have for the storage units near The Colonnades. Is that where you kept our paintings for art class Scott?' said Carla.

'It does. What's the number,' Scott asked.

'127.'

'Yeah, that's one of ours.'

'Won't it be closed? The art would be thrown out or, sold or something?' said Brady.

'Oh no,' said Scott, 'I pay for storage for the art students. We have several units. I had no idea Scarlett's art was there. Knock me down with a feather. What a find, though.'

'Don't you keep records on the units and the numbers?' Neville looked stunned.

'No, Sherlock, I don't. Maybe now, I'll let *you* organise me. But only if...'

'If what?'

'If you leave teaching, look after me and write full time.'

'We've been through all that.' Neville glared at Scott.

'When can we take a look?' squealed Ebony. 'Sorry to interrupt.'

'Don't pester, Ebony,' said Brady. He pulled a piece of paper from the purse.'

'What's that Dad?'

'It's your mother's writing. It looks like a poem.'

'Really, let me see.' Ebony reached for the paper, but Brady held it, reluctant to look.

'I don't know.' Brady's eyes clouded. 'It's called "Between".'

'Oh,' said Scott, 'I remember that. I made everyone

write a short piece to go with an art piece for homework. Scarlett didn't want to read hers out, but she did the painting.'

'It was my idea. The writing thing.' said Neville. 'Anyway we should be going.'

'Yes,' said Carla, 'me too. Jeff and the boys will wonder if I've skipped the country.' She gave Ebony a warm hug. 'Remember to come and visit. Both of you.'

After everyone had said their goodbyes, Ebony picked up the poem.

'Read it out loud Eb, I love hearing you read.'

'Okay, Dad, here goes,.

"Between,

How high is up?
a mountain?
a spaceship?
Heaven?

How low is down?
a valley?
an ocean?
Hell?

Why can't I live
between the two
never at one
or the other.

Just between.

Not winter
or summer
but autumn
or spring
Between".'

Ebony's eyes misted. 'Wow, Dad, it's lovely, but kinda sad

too. I don't know what it means.'

'I guess,' Brady said, 'your mother was between the earth and the sky, between heaven and hell, between joy and sadness, truth and lies. Between living and dying, I guess.'

'We didn't get many answers today, did we?'

'Sure we did, Eb. Your mother was struggling. She loved us. She left us her paintings, for when we were ready.'

'Can we have an exhibition? A celebration, you know, of her life. I'll read the poem. Maybe Carla...the gallery?'

'You're brilliant Eb, did I ever tell you...Your mother would be very proud.'

'I just wish she could be there, be here.' Ebony leant her head on her father's shoulder.

'Oh, darling. If there's a window in heaven, your mother will find it, and be there. After all, she was on her way home to us.'

Carnage

'Eccles, come back here! Really Neville, why did you bring that elephant of a dog?' Scott scowled. 'And you're late, Nev.'

Scott was sitting in the café area of Carla's gallery, that was on their McLaren Vale property, enjoying a tall iced coffee with Carla, her husband Jeff, and Jack and Helen, who'd helped transport the art. Neville had been catching up on marking assignments.

'It's okay.' Carla laughed, attempting to ward off the enthusiastic dog. 'Jeff, call the boys and get them to take Eccles for a run in the top paddock.'

'You were the one who phoned and told me to come straight over, Scott. What was I supposed to do with Eccles? Be reasonable, love,' Neville said. 'Anyway you've finished with the paintings haven't you?'

'Whatever.' Scott gave a weary sigh. 'The paintings are safely stored in the back room of Carla's gallery, safe from that mutt, thank goodness.'

Jeff summoned the boys who were only too happy to

have a romp with the St Bernard. They took off laughing across the grassy field.

'Well, introduce me,' said Neville, shading a hand to look at Jeff.

'Sorry,' said Carla.

'Take no notice of him, Carla. He's a drama queen,' said Scott.

Carla smiled, 'This is my husband Jeff,' she said. And these two are Jack and Helena. They helped transport the art.'

'Gosh, you're going to be a big boy when you grow up, Jack!' said Neville. 'Bet they made you carry everything.'

Jack laughed.

'Neville!' said Scott. 'Sorry, I can't take him anywhere.'

'What's wrong? The man's built like a tank.' Neville turned to Jack. 'Are you an ex-rugby player or a copper?'

'Ex-cop,' said Jack, leaning languidly back in his chair. 'But don't hold that against me.'

'This is a gorgeous area, Carla,' said Neville. 'Is this where you're thinking of having the exhibition of Scarlett's art?'

'Yes,' said Carla, 'why don't you take Neville to have a look, Scott.'

The sails sheltering the café flapped rhythmically in the warm summer breeze. Leaves skittered across the paved courtyard. Jack and Helena turned to each other and began to chat in low voices.

'Cute pair those two,' said Carla, smiling. 'Jeff, tell your father to come and be sociable.'

'I tried,' said Jeff. 'He's taking a moment.'

'Typical,' said Carla, frowning.

Jeff frowned. 'Dad's here visiting. He's just retired, he was a GP in his own practice. He and Mum have split up. Mum threw him out of the house. She won't speak to him and neither will my sister. He has nowhere to go, so he's staying here.'

'*Temporarily*,' said Carla.

'Dad and Carla don't see eye to eye.' Jeff shrugged.

Carla rolled her eyes. 'Women see things men don't see about each other.'

'What does that mean?'

'Never mind. Maybe he'll be over his "moment" later when we go inside for coffee.'

'Go on, Ebony,' said Brady, ruffling his daughter's hair. 'She's been busting to give you the purse, Carla. She can't wait to have it repaired. Thanks for sorting that.'

Ebony leaned eagerly forward and handed Carla the purse.

Carla accepted it and inspected the stitching. 'It will need a new lining,' she said, idly pulling threads. The lining came apart with ease. 'Oh my, there's a photograph in here.' She removed a small photograph. 'It's an ultrasound. How adorable, it must be you Ebony.' She placed it in Ebony's eager fingers.

'Oh, wow, that's so special,' said Ebony. 'Hang on…'

'What's wrong Eb?' Brady asked.

'It's not me. It's 1991.'

'Show me,' Brady said, taking the image. 'There's some sort of mistake. It must be someone else's photo.'

'It says Scarlett Camberwell,' said Ebony, her voice flat. '16 weeks' gestation.'

'What! That can't be right,' said Carla. 'That was when she attempted suicide.'

'No,' said Jeff, shifting uncomfortably in his seat. 'It wasn't.' All eyes turned to him.

'What do you know about this, Jeff?' Carla folded her arms, her eyes fiery.

'No one was supposed to know. God, this is hard. Scarlett swore me to secrecy. She was frantic when she found out she was pregnant. She wouldn't tell anyone who the father was, and believe me her parents tried. Dad was her GP and referred her to a gynaecologist. She had an abortion. Dad offered to take her to the hospital, but she wouldn't let him.'

'Who took her?'

'Her parents. They were devastated.'

'So she never attempted suicide?' Brady asked.

'No, people assumed that, and it seemed better to let them believe it.'

'Better for who?' Carla's voice rose. 'Why didn't you tell me?'

'Please don't take this out on me, Carla. Remember we were only fifteen too. I only found out because I overheard Dad making the appointment on the phone. I talked to Scarlett and she said if anyone knew, she'd kill herself. I was a kid.'

'Oh my God,' said Scott. The others turned to see the shocked faces of Neville and Scott.

Brady stood and walked away. Ebony ran to him.

'We'll leave,' said Neville, 'this is personal.'

'We can't yet,' said Scott, 'the dog.'

Brady turned. 'I wouldn't mind a word with your father, Jeff.' His voice was cold, forbidding. 'And I'd like everyone there. It hardly matters now.'

Jack leapt to his feet. 'Okay. Let's go inside. You can introduce everyone to your father, Jeff. Let's meet Dr...What's his name?'

'Emery Dunne,' said Jeff, defeated. 'Dr Emery Dunne.'

A slender balding man was washing up in the sink when the bulk of Jack Bragg blocked the door as he entered. 'Dr Dunne, I presume.'

'Call me Emery,' said the man, approaching with his hand extended.

Jack's expression was bland as he shook the man's hand firmly.

Emery winced. 'Quite a grip, mate,' he said, rubbing his hand.

Jack stood aside to let the others enter. He leaned

against a wall, his eyes narrow and assessing.

Brady came next, his face like thunder.

Ebony walked into the room and the blood drained from Emery's face as he stumbled back against the bench. He didn't notice Scott and Neville enter, or see Helena at the door.

'Dad, are you okay?' Jeff stepped towards his father.

'What the hell? Who?'

'Scarlett's daughter. You remember the Camberwells,' Jeff said.

Emery Dunne wasn't listening. He continued to stare at Ebony in shock.

'No! Scarlett got rid of it! I know, I sent her to Peterson, the gynaecologist. Don't tell me she didn't go through with it. What are you trying to pull?'

'Dad! What's your problem?'

'And you, Carla. I suppose you had a nice chat to Scarlett. Best friends and all. A chat about the painting. That's what started it wasn't it. That bloody portrait. I just wanted to buy it, it meant nothing. I don't know why she reacted.'

'The portrait. That's what Scarlett was talking about. She didn't say "Everyone wants to buy the painting" she said "Emery Dunne wants to buy the painting". She didn't want you to have it.'

'My God,' said Scott, 'That's why she was upset about the thing. You're the jerk that frightened her.' The memory of Scarlett on the night she fled flashed into his mind. 'You prick! You have no idea. I should hit your smug face.'

Neville rested his hand on Scott's shoulder. 'Chill, love.'

Emery threw his hands up. 'I don't believe this. I don't need two poofs putting their oar in.'

'I've changed my mind,' said Neville. 'Hit his smug face, Scott.'

Brady moved towards Emery. 'This isn't about the painting.' His voice was so cold and low that the room stilled. 'This is about a pregnant fifteen year old girl.'

'Who are you? Why don't you mind your business?' Emery glared at Brady.

'I am minding my own business. And I'm your worst nightmare, Dr Emery Dunne. That's who I am.'

'It's lies. It wasn't mine. I wasn't the father, I don't care what anyone says.' Emery leaned forward and jabbed a belligerent finger at Jeff.

'Dad, what the hell? You're losing it.' Jeff turned to Carla. Her face was pale with shock.

Emery saw the image of the ultrasound in Ebony's hand. 'I won't have a DNA test. I won't. It's all lies! Lies, I tell you!' He leaned forward.

Neville put his hand over his mouth to stifle a shriek.

Ebony whimpered and shrunk against Brady. He circled her with his arms. 'What's going on, Dad?'

'Here darling,' said Helena, stepping forward to embrace Ebony. 'Let your father sort this.'

Emery stepped towards Jeff, his hands out in supplication. 'Son, you know me. Don't you dare get this wrong!'

Jack took a step forward and this small act stilled Emery's advance into the room.

Jeff's face distorted. 'Carla never knew Scarlett was pregnant. Only you, Dad. Only you and the Camberwells. I overheard you on the phone organising the abortion, but no-one else knew.'

For moments the room seemed airless. Then like a falling deck of cards, the truth began to sink in, replacing the shock.

Emery scowled like a cornered animal. Red splotches of colour appeared on his face. He continued to stare at Ebony.

'She's not yours,' said Brady, fists clenched.

'But I thought…' said Emery.

'You filthy creature.' Carla glared at Emery, flushed with anger. 'You! Scarlett was only fifteen.'

'You, Dad?' Jeff took another step. 'Scarlett wouldn't tell me who the father was. But it was you, wasn't it? All those trips home after babysitting.'

'Don't listen to Carla's lies, son. The little bitch will say anything. She'll probably accuse me too.'

Jeff lunged. 'You bastard!'

Jack intercepted Jeff, deftly lifting Emery by the back of his jacket. He carried him down the stairs and deposited him at the bottom in a heap.

'Don't move,' Jack said. 'I'll phone a taxi,'

'Get your hands off me, you ignorant mountain.' Emery stood and straightened his clothes. 'I don't want a bloody taxi.'

'Trust me,' said Jack. 'It'll be better than an ambulance, Sunshine.'

Goodbye Elise

'Dad, can you believe it's been a year since we left Sydney?' Ebony peered from the plane window. 'The ocean is lighter here. I guess because it's the Pacific, not the Southern Ocean.'

'That's funny,' said Brady, 'that's the first thing I noticed when I arrived in Sydney.'

'We're probably imagining it you know, it's all the same water.' The plane was landing. Ebony slipped her handbag under the seat in front. 'It's hard to believe Grandma Camberwell won't be there. A stroke, gone so fast. She looked fine, back then, before we moved.'

'Things change. You okay, Eb?'

'Yeah, I am, I mean I'm sad, but I'm okay. I was actually just thinking how much we've changed. You and I. A year ago you would have protected me from this, and now we're travelling together. Facing this together. Just the two of us.'

Brady cleared his throat. 'You're not a kid anymore. So you've forgiven me for transplanting you?'

Ebony smiled. 'I really didn't want to tell you this until I was at least 30, but it's been the best thing that happened. For everyone.'

A chauffeur held up a card with Brady and Ebony's names. He approached with professional civility and reached for their bags 'Is this all, sir? Miss?'

A chill wind chased papers outside the comfort of the airport, but it had little chance to penetrate the new arrivals.

A black salon car was parked near the large glass exit doors. The chauffeur opened the car doors, eyes fixed on the distance.

Ebony shot her father a glance. She'd forgotten about the privilege and wealth of her grandparents. Perhaps she'd never really been a part of it, thanks to her parents. She was relieved. There was something cold and solemn about it, detached.

A maid ushered them in. Tony Camberwell came to greet them, his body stooped. There was more grey in his hair. He looked years older. Ebony's heart clenched.

There was discreet bustle around them, staff Ebony didn't know, serenely doing things she didn't remember. Luggage taken, trays of drinks. Had it really been like this? Had her mother Scarlett lived like this?

'Didn't bring much. Not staying long then.' Tony Camberwell gave her a hug. His movements were stiff, he was thinner. 'Lovely to see you Ebony.'

'Great to see you too, Grandpa.' Ebony stole a look at her father. He was watching her in taut silence.

'Give that bag to the maid, Brady.' Tony indicated a woman standing a little behind him. Brady relinquished the bag with a grim smile and a 'thank you'.

Tony gave him a sharp look. He preferred the servants to remain invisible. 'You must both be hungry. I'll tell the cook to plate up.'

With urbane politeness, Tony asked about Ebony's school, Brady's job, the older Harcourts, then the conversation lagged. The large dining room was cold and dim, being in the centre of the house where no natural light intruded. The chink of silver on porcelain seemed to echo. Ebony wriggled.

'You look tired, are you okay, Ebony?

'Yes, no, I mean...I'm fine, Grandpa.'

'Well, if you're finished you can scoot on up to bed. There's a television in your room. I'd like to talk to your dad.'

Ebony paled.

'Ebony's okay to stay, Tony.' Brady wiped a serviette across his lips and placed it down with a decisive tap.

'It's an adult conversation, Brady.' Tony dropped his knife and scraped his chair back.

'It's okay, Dad.' Ebony slid from the chair and headed upstairs.

'You can sit down Brady.' Tony leant back in the armchair.

Ebony took off her shoes and tip-toed back down the carpeted stairs and huddled at the bottom of the stairs.

'I don't like you excluding Ebony, Tony.'

'She's just a kid, Brady.' Tony's eyes darkened.

'She's sixteen, Tony.'

'Like I said, a kid. Anyway, what I have to say is for you alone. Come on man, why won't you sit down?'

Brady leaned against the door jamb.

Tony threw up his hands. 'All right, have it your way. I know you and Ebony are, what do the kids say? "tight"— that whole the-two-of-us-against-the-world thing you've always had going on, excluding Scarlett...'

'Now come on Tony, that's not fair and you know it.'

'Don't pretend with me, Brady. I saw how my daughter was cut off, left out.'

Ebony shivered and hugged the wall.

'That's not true. Scarlett's condition alienated her, not us. Not any of us, it wasn't anyone's fault.'

'Don't patronise me, Brady. I knew my daughter. And I saw what was happening.'

'That's rich, that is.' Brady took in a deep breath. He sliced the air with a hand. 'Now is not the time, Tony. I will not discuss this now. We'll talk after the funeral. And Ebony will be there to participate if she chooses.'

'There isn't a funeral.'

'What? Excuse me? What are you talking about?'

'We *had* the funeral. Days ago, just Elise's sisters. Only a small affair. That's how things are done now. It's what...'

'And you didn't think to tell us that!'

'What difference does it make to you how things are done? Whether there's a huge gathering or not?'

'This isn't about the way you do things. That's your choice. None of this is about...I can't believe this, Tony. You just don't get it, do you?' Brady's voice cracked as he lowered himself into a lounge chair.

The room grew silent. Brady didn't trust himself to speak. There was a chasm in the room, a murky distance between the two men. The dishwasher whirred. The grandfather clock in the hall tick-tocked the seconds.

'Scarlett adored you, you know. Worshipped you. It was love at first sight. She said you were her Zhivago, the other half of her very self, the piece that was missing.'

'And I loved her, but no one can be all that, Tony. Don't you see?' Brady placed his hands palms up.

Ebony wept silently against the wall, wiping her eyes with her sleeve. She heard her father torn between condemnation and compassion.

'You didn't appreciate what you had. A love that pure and true...'

'Tony, you're full of shit. There was nothing true about the lie you lived, the lie you made Scarlett live.'

'What the hell? How dare you. I don't know what...'

'The abortion, Tony. Passing it off as a suicide attempt,

letting Scarlett live that lie. Not just at fifteen, but the rest of her life. That's what I'm talking about. I can't make it any clearer.'

'That was Scarlett's choice. She was ashamed.'

'She didn't need to be ashamed, not with me, never with me. The anguish she must have suffered, the sheer needless pain of keeping all that hidden. I never had the chance to tell her it made no difference to me. The lie did more harm than the cover up ever could. I wish you understood that, Tony. There was no shame. God, I loved her. I loved her courage and her vitality. And yes, I cherish the fact that she loved only me. Loved me best and last.'

'She was fragile.'

'She was a warrior. She faced more demons than you or I know. She didn't need to run away from the past as well. We could have faced it, together. All of us.'

But Tony was no longer listening, no longer in the present. His eyes were moist as he stared at the gathering shroud of night. His voice was defeated, a tired whisper. 'You were supposed to save her.'

Celebration

The melody of a string quartet was carried by the Southerly breeze that brought relief from the humid evening air.

Dusk was falling. Clouds that had earlier threatened rain, now served to add spectacular depth to a sienna sunset. Golden rays of the dying sun made a glorious backdrop.

'Is there going to be any decent dancing music, Dad?'

'This is dancing music, Eb.' Brady gathered his daughter into a slow waltz. 'You're not disappointed about cancelling the exhibition?'

'No, Dad. This is better, a small party with friends. I don't think I could have handled it. Not after the drama with that … that man.'

'It's over now. We'll never have to see him again.'

'We certainly got answers. More than we bargained for.' Ebony leant her head on Brady's shoulder. 'Thanks for helping me decide what to do with Mum's paintings. I love the portrait. It will always remind me of Mum, regardless of the mess. And I'm fine with letting Carla sell the paintings we don't want at the gallery.'

The quartet finished the piece.

'You going to dance with Emma, Dad? I don't want you to ignore her.'

'Oh, I'm going to do a lot more than that.' Brady grinned.

Jenna walked over to the quartet and waited while they ruffled new music sheets.

'What's Jenna doing, Dad?'

'She's going to sing, Eb.'

'Sing?'

'Yes, sweetie. I believe it's usual for someone to sing at a wedding.' Brady winked.

Ebony swung around to search the group for Emma. She stood poised with her arm linked through Iris's.

'Dad! You wretch. I don't believe you've done this.'

'Believe it, kiddo. I'm getting married. We'd better make tracks to the front. After all, you promised to be my best man, remember?' Brady curved his arm under hers and led her to the front beside the quartet. Iris joined them and turned to smile at her daughter.

'Why didn't you tell me?' whispered Ebony.

'I couldn't stand the thought of you in coat and tails.'

Ebony slapped him. 'You hate surprises.'

'But I'm not surprised.'

The quartet began to play. Emma came towards them

with an armful of November lilies. Brady beamed.

'I hope Jenna can sing,' said Ebony.

'So do I, kiddo.'

www.ingramcontent.com/pod-product-compliance
Lightning Source LLC
Chambersburg PA
CBHW012001120726
47901CB00012BA/2540